MURDER IN A NUNNERY

*On the steps of St. Joseph's altar lay
the corpulent body of the Baroness
Sliema — still, so it seemed to the
horrified nuns, heaving under the blow
which had struck her down . . .* Chief
Inspector Pearson of Scotland Yard is
called in to solve the crime — but the
old wealthy Baroness had quarrelled
with most everyone in Harrington Convent, and there is no shortage of suspects.
What's more, he must deal with a particularly shrewd Reverend Mother, and
nuns and students who lead him on a
merry chase . . .

D1077008

ERIC SHEPHERD

MURDER IN A NUNNERY

Complete and Unabridged

LINFORD
Leicester

First published in Great Britain in 1940

First Linford Edition
published 2018

Copyright © 1940 by Eric Shepherd
All rights reserved

A catalogue record for this book is available
from the British Library.

ISBN 978–1–4448–3922–7

Published by
F. A. Thorpe (Publishing)
Anstey, Leicestershire

Set by Words & Graphics Ltd.
Anstey, Leicestershire
Printed and bound in Great Britain by
T. J. International Ltd., Padstow, Cornwall

This book is printed on acid-free paper

Author's Note

Every book must take its chance, but an author is entitled to resent any imputation of being too dull to invent the persons and places required to eke out his fictions. In this story persons, places, in fact the whole box of tricks, are purely imaginary. There is neither bus nor train to Harrington Convent, and the other name of every character in it is Harris.

Stories often arise out of holiday talk. There was once a holiday party in Baslow, Derbyshire, consisting of the author, his wife, David, John, Teresa, Catherine, and Magdalen. There were also Kenneth, Sissy, and Janny. The surroundings would have been congruous in Eden, but the conversation often turned on the darker and messier consequences of the Fall, and it was there that this little story began to take shape. The author would like to commemorate a happy occasion and associate again all the charming people who took part in it by inscribing to each and all of them, with his love, *Murder in a Nunnery*.

1

VERITY IS LATE, AND SO, IN ANOTHER SENSE, IS THE OLD BARONESS

Towards the hour of Benediction on a bright, warm afternoon of May.

The bell announcing this ceremony already ringing out over garden and playing-fields summoning the girls of Harrington Convent School to their evening devotions.

Up every path and round every clump of bushes groups of them coming in their summer uniforms, some of them showing but little alacrity and being pounced on by Mother Peagle, a brisk, alert little nun whose job it is to round up stragglers and apply the spur.

'Now then, children, hurry, hurry. Hurry now, or you will be late. And you know what Reverend Mother thinks of loiterers!'

Her voice, though urgent, is not at all sharp; it is like the genial barking of a sheepdog.

Next minute, by an exercise of that disconcerting gift of hers, famous throughout Harrington, Mother Peagle is somewhere else, quite a long way off, exhorting another group of slowcoaches.

Mother Peagle being safely out of hearing, Miss Verity Goodchild, a tall girl of fifteen, gives vent to her feelings among her friends.

'Oh dear,' she laments, tossing her fair hair from side to side after a habit of hers much discouraged by authority, 'oh *dear*, I am so bored! I feel like breaking out and doing something desperate! If something doesn't happen in this dead-alive hole before to-morrow morning I shall — I shall . . . '

Prudence Rockingham, a girl adorned from shoulder to hip with the Blue Ribbon of a prefect, interrupts with one of those soft answers studiously calculated not to turn away wrath.

'Something *will* happen, my dear, if you're late for Benediction. You remember the frightful blowing-up Reverend Mother gave us about punctuality in chapel? . . . '

'Would you deny the politeness of earthly kings to the King of kings?' murmurs Philomene Watts, quoting apparently from the spirited address in question. Philomene, Verity's closest friend, is a slight, pale, deceptively demure girl.

Verity utters a real Old Testament groan — another of her many discouraged accomplishments — and allows herself to be pulled along faster, for already the organ can be heard tuning up for the Entrance Hymn under the plump hands of Mother Frederica.

Some minutes later, a numerous choir of young angels, all veiled in white, enters the chapel in procession and passes down the central aisle, praising the bridal altar of May with a hymn of heart-breaking sweetness.

In their stalls at the back kneel the nuns in their gracious weeds, presided over by Reverend Mother.

The voice of Mother Peagle can still be heard from without even above the singing — still admonishing . . .

Tap-tap, tap-tap-tap! All the girls know what *that* is, and some of the more graceless make faces and even put out tongues under discreet cover of their veils. The Junior School, seated forward, can *see* what it is, even if they did not know. It is Harrington's lady-boarder, old Baroness Sliema, tapping a cautious way with her ebony cane to her special prie-dieu in the dusk of St. Joseph's chapel, followed by her dumpy, always breathless, little companion, Mrs. Moss. Both wear *mantillas* of black lace, the Baroness's a sumptuous heirloom of an affair suggesting the Catholic majesty of old Madrid. Tall, stout, and of ponderous weight though the Baroness is, she leans heavily and as if possessively on her distressed companion, and requires assistance to lower her bulk on to the crimson faldstool, where she plops down with fat shoulders heaving. Mrs. Moss, more breathless than ever, subsides faintly into the background.

The Junior School exchanges angry glances and suppresses a desire to hiss.

4

But the knowledgeable among them (and this is the majority!) steal a glance at the young lay-teacher of languages, Miss Venetia Gozo, who has just entered the chapel of Our Lady and directed, as she genuflects, a look of sheer hate out of her luscious black eyes at the old Baroness and her proceedings.

Glances — and even nudges — are again exchanged. It is known in the school that Miss Gozo is the ward of the old Baroness, and this fact is charitably held to excuse the young woman's quick temper and tartness in class.

'Poor wretch!' is the general opinion of the school; and there are long and wordy disputes as to whether the obviously un-English Miss Gozo is pretty or not.

But now, sumptuously coped in shimmering white brocade, the priest has approached the altar, attended by a small seraph tossing a bowl of incense. The priest has opened the Tabernacle door amid the blazing candles, and profoundly genuflected. Mother Vannes from her sacristy has floodlit the gracious scene; and, as the Sacred Host is mounted in the monstrance, all voices are raised — from that of Reverend Mother herself down to the shrill pipe of Thistle McBinkie, the youngest child in the school — in the hymn of loving and triumphant greeting —

O salutaris Hostia . . .

There is a slight rustling noise halfway down the aisle, and quick footsteps muted to the utmost!

Prudence Rockingham and Philomene Watts well know what it is, and make room beside them for a flushed and breathless Verity Goodchild as with ill-adjusted veil she wraps herself in belated prayer.

In spite of all Mother Peagle's efforts Verity has been unable to find that veil, has mislaid her prayer-book, and is late!

Although she has waited outside the door until that acceptable season when Reverend Mother is likely to be preoccupied with devotion, none the less she has felt that all-seeing eye boring into the small of her back; and she knows too well that, in spite of the kindly intercession of Mother Peagle, she will be sent for by Reverend Mother into her parlour as soon as Benediction is over . . .

And not the first time this term either!

Low on her knees, her face hidden on her arms, Verity bethinks herself desperately what saint to pray to — which of all that Holy Communion in Heaven has a lingering weakness for delinquent schoolgirls? . . .

She cannot think.

But Philomene Watts, under cover of the resounding *Tantum ergo* now struck up, prompts her in a whisper.

'Have a go at St. Joseph, Verity. He's an awful decent old bird all round . . . '

With a gesture of gratitude Verity prostrates herself in spirit at the feet of the Patron of the Universal Church, and so do Philomene and Prudence in support of their unhappy friend.

Laudate Dominum — chants the choir: *Laudate eum omnes populi* . . .

It sounds rather unfeeling to Verity — and definitely premature. She shuts her eyes very tight and pegs away at the

Litany of St. Joseph:

Joseph justissime
Joseph fidelissime
Custos virginum
Terror daemonium

Some of the invocations amaze her with their aptness.

But none the less, as the procession of girls hymns its way from the chapel, Verity feels a light tap on the arm and beholds the figure of Mother Peagle detaining her, much more in sorrow than in anger.

'Oh, Verity, my child; how could you be so late!'

'It was my veil, Mother; truly it was. I couldn't find the — the thing . . . '

'I am afraid it was your carelessness. You had better go back into the chapel and say a special prayer, for Reverend Mother wants to see you in her parlour in five minutes' time.'

'Oh, *Mother!* . . . '

But Mother Peagle only urges haste so as to have as much time as possible for prayer.

Sadly Verity acts on the good advice, murmuring sorrowfully to herself as she goes:

'St. Joseph seems off his stroke this afternoon, but I suppose I'd better go on with him as I've started.'

The deserted chapel is now in semi-darkness, its usual state when no service is in progress. The candles have all been extinguished. What light there is comes from the narrow windows hidden away above the altar, and from the seven crimson lamps denoting the Blessed Sacrament.

Verity kneels far down, in the places recently vacated by Thistle McBinkie and her small coevals.

'Oh blessed St. Joseph,' prays Verity, 'do be a dear. You know as well as I do that it really wasn't my fault. Some beast had hidden my veil. Do unharden Reverend Mother's heart, O Terror of Demons . . . or make her have a very important engagement. She might forget; she sometimes does, you know. Mother Peagle won't remind her if she does, so those are the lines to work on, O

Guardian of Virgins . . . though of course if you can think of anything better . . . '

In the fervour of her petition Verity raised her eyes and looked the tall image of St. Joseph full in the face.

'Be a sport,' she added.

But then happened the most extraordinary thing which had ever happened in that chapel, and its echoes shuddered with a shrill and horrified scream!

Mother Vannes rushed across from the sacristy — omitting for the first and only time in her life to genuflect; while the ever-watchful Mother Peagle — if the expression is permissible — positively *sprinted* down the aisle. Between them they raised the stricken Verity, who, white as a sheet, had fallen over sideways in a heap and was churning the flimsy pages of innumerable prayer-books with her legs.

'Verity; my child! What is it? . . . '

But Verity could only cling to them and point. Her trembling finger seemed to accuse St. Joseph himself standing larger than life in the dusk of his chapel. At first the nuns could see nothing unusual, but then Mother Vannes, with a smothered cry, sprang to the marble rail, dragging Mother Peagle with her.

'Dear God have mercy on us! Look . . . '

Agitated, and by some mischance without her glasses, Mother Peagle strained her eyes beyond the pale tip of the pointing finger. Vision and extreme horror were vouchsafed her together.

'The blessed Saints protect us! . . . '

On the steps of St. Joseph's altar, toppled in a heap from the faldstool, lay the corpulent body of the Baroness Sliema — still, so it seemed to the horrified nuns, heaving under the blow which had struck her down.

By the crimson light of the sacred lamps glowing so serenely they could see the blood welling, and, jutting forth from the ribs at an angle which seemed to denote scorn, the glint of the knife which had stabbed her . . .

2

SO THIS IS A NUNNERY!

No sooner was Reverend Mother made aware that murder had been committed on the conventual premises than she acted, and on the principle of first things first and all things in order.

Fr. Witherstick, S. J., of the neighbouring Jesuit House, was informed by telephone that the most atrocious sacrilege had defiled the chapel, and would he come round without loss of a minute to remove the Sacred Elements elsewhere. Fr. Witherstick was on the doorstep five minutes later, and, assisted by Reverend Mother and some of the senior nuns, had performed the solemn translation.

The Novices under their Mistress, and some of the junior nuns, were then told to keep watch in the improvised sanctuary, making constant Acts of Reparation — and from this exercise they were by no means to desist until Reverend Mother gave the word. Thus a possibly hysterical section of the Community was disposed of to advantage.

The school, under Mother Peagle and her assistants, was assembled together, where Reverend Mother informed them in the most casual voice what had happened, afterwards handing them over to Fr. Witherstick to be given a long instruction on an abstruse point of doctrine.

Many of the children fell fast asleep, which was exactly what Reverend Mother had aimed at.

The police were then notified.

'Hell's bells!' exclaimed Detective-Sergeant Osbert among his colleagues at the local station; 'but here's a tit-bit to write home to mother! Nun been walled up or something over at Harrington! Ring the Coroner, one of you, and let's get down there.'

Immediately afterwards the Detective-Sergeant, Police-Surgeon Goodall and several constables, left by car for the Convent.

But if these gentlemen had been disposed to find something funny in the idea of a murder in a Nunnery they were soon called to order and made to think very differently when they encountered Mother Peck, the portress, at the door. Mother Peck looked them over with a sharp and blighting eye, dwelling particularly on their feet — and then interned them in a small and hideous parlour designed to break the contentious spirit of visiting parents. Here she left them — with a supply of C.T.S. tracts — until, as she put it, 'someone had time to attend to them.'

She then departed, and the police officers exchanged glances rather like 'stout Cortez' on his peak. This sort of treatment accorded very ill with the dignity of the Law. They had expected to find the whole place full of swooning nuns and girls whom they would reassure with their manly presence . . . 'Now then, ladies, no reason for alarm; let me beg of you . . . ' But it was all quite different, and here was their manly presence shut up in an ugly little parlour under the compulsion of a peremptory little nun about the size and general figure of cock-robin.

'Well, I'm jiggered,' exclaimed the Detective-Sergeant; and Dr. Goodall had even got so far as to open the door of the parlour when a sneeze unmistakably from the nose of Mother Peck in the lodge caused him to shut it again with a guilty look.

It was Reverend Mother's deliberate policy always to remain in the background as long as ever she could, and so it was the gracious figure of a certain Mother Trevor which ultimately came to the rescue of the imprisoned police. But she did not come until Dr. Goodall for sheer want of other occupation had read through a C.T.S. pamphlet on Matrimony, with every word of which he cholerically disagreed. But he never made any of the cutting remarks he had intended, nor did the Detective-Sergeant lodge the official complaint, for the presence of Mother Trevor made it impossible to be anything but polite and deferential.

She spoke with calm and grave sweetness.

'We are so sorry to have kept you gentlemen waiting, but Reverend Mother begs you to excuse us. We have been so busy with emergency arrangements for the children and younger nuns . . . you will understand?'

The Detective-Sergeant, out of sheer force of professional habit, contrived to look as if this story did not convince *him*; but Dr. Goodall was on his feet bowing and clicking heels with a Continental courtesy.

'Your arrangements, Madam, appear to have been highly successful . . . '

Mother Trevor sighed.

'We have done our best. But such a thing, coming right in the middle of term . . . I can only say that whoever did it showed very little consideration for Reverend Mother's feelings . . . '

It was plain that to this gentle lady the thoughtlessness of the crime was quite its most striking feature.

The Coroner's officer being now in attendance, the body of the old Baroness

16

was removed to a suitable place, where Dr. Goodall and the Convent's medical adviser were soon chatting cheerfully over post-mortem phenomena.

It was all very well for the medicos, their job was a mere matter of routine; but the Detective-Sergeant was soon a very much bewildered man. A mere tour of the interior premises tired him out. The nuns were all dressed identically alike; all moved soundlessly about, demure and self-effacing, hugging the wall and never raising the eyes unnecessarily. They gave polite and intelligent answers to questions, but — some of them spoke no English!

Then there was the school — miles of *it*, and swarms of *them*; again all much alike.

'I suppose,' he said to Mother Trevor, 'we can pretty well rule out the youngsters, eh, Madam?'

But Mother Trevor, with that faintly worried look of hers, could not suppose anything of the kind.

'Oh no, I don't think you can do that. I will speak to Reverend Mother. But you must remember we are a very cosmopolitan school — very; we have children from all over the world. Some of the countries one cannot even pronounce. I am afraid it would be rash to assume that none of the children has ever knifed anybody.'

The detective's hair rose slightly on his head, but the quiet voice flowed on.

'It is not for us to judge of other peoples, and one realizes that nursery customs differ greatly in different countries. I am sure they all mean well, poor little things — and many of them set an example to us nuns in the fervour of their piety. We have one child, little Inez Escapado, who comes to us from Anaconda . . . when we first had her she was wearing the blessed scapular of Our Lady and a dagger down her poor little stocking. It took Reverend Mother *hours* of patient persuasion to get the child to part with the dagger. Apparently all the little girls in Anaconda wear daggers.'

Again the listener's scalp contracted, but he managed to ask:

'And have you many children brought up in this way?'

Mother Trevor seemed lost in a reckoning process.

'Oh not *many* . . . at least, as to daggers. But I believe Reverend Mother had to remove a rather dangerous *pistol* from under the pillow of dear little Grazia Bombado, our little Corsican. She did not seem able to fall happily off to sleep without her pistol. Such a sweet child — with a quite special devotion to the Nine Fridays . . . '

'To the — *what*, Madam?'

It sounded to the detective like some subtle way of administering poison over a period!

Mother Trevor suppressed a sigh; she, too, was finding it a strain to talk to a person who seemed ignorant of the most elementary things. But she brightened up as the reason for this occurred to her.

'But of course; I was forgetting you are a Protestant. Poor you! . . . '

She hastened to add:

'Not but what there are many, many saintly souls among the Protestants. I am sure many of them live far holier lives than we do. As Reverend Mother put it in

19

a recent Conference, — after all, what are they to do but go on being good Protestants if they do not receive the grace to become good Catholics?'

Detective-Sergeant Osbert felt a whirling sensation in the head. He could make nothing of these dignified quietly spoken ladies in their uniform bonnets and draperies who seemed to be quite undisturbed by a mere murder. His heart quailed at the prospect of an investigation involving young children with daggers and pistols and queer partialities for days of the week. A resolution was forming in his mind . . . The Yard must be got in on this without loss of time. He must ring up local headquarters for permission to call in the Yard.

But for his craven terror of Mother Peck mounting guard over the telephone-room, he would have put the matter through immediately. But he was realizing that not even a policeman can do exactly what he pleases in a Convent, so he addressed himself humbly to Mother Trevor.

'I should like to use the telephone. I

think this case is a matter for the Yard . . . '

It was clear to him that Mother Trevor had not the faintest idea what the 'Yard' was, but she inclined her head sympathetically.

'But I am afraid,' he added sadly, 'that the holy Mother at the door doesn't like me very much.'

'Oh yes, she does,' Mother Trevor answered tranquilly; 'it is only her manner. I do not think there is anybody Mother Peck dislikes. She is charity itself, and the dearest, most zealous soul! She would go through fire and water for Reverend Mother . . . and such a favourite with the Archbishop . . . '

There is no accounting for tastes, the detective thought as he followed Mother Trevor to the lodge.

But at sight of Mother Trevor the irate eye of Mother Peck softened to a genial beam.

'What can I have the pleasure of doing for you, Mother?'

'It is this gentleman. He has come here about the murder. You know . . . the murder which took place this afternoon . . . '

Mother Peck nodded, with the air of one recalling a thing of small importance.

'And I understand,' pursued Mother Trevor, 'that he wishes to use the telephone, with your kind permission . . . '

Mother Peck smiled at her, most affable and obliging.

'Certainly, Mother. Let him come with me and I will show him how.'

3

THE YARD ARRIVES
AT HARRINGTON

So urgent must have been the local S O S to Scotland Yard that, scarcely more than an hour later, a police car pulled up in Harrington Lane opposite the Convent door, and out of it stepped a person who might very easily have been mistaken for a clergyman of the vanishing evangelical type. A single glance at him suggested Tennyson's memorable line

That good man, the clergyman —

if it did not go even further and recall Wordsworth's equally famous line

A Mr. Wilkinson, a clergyman.

It was in fact Chief-Inspector Andrew William Pearson of the Yard.

Regarded as a detective, the Chief Inspector might be said to have been born in disguise; his mother had seen to her child's due provision in this respect. There was nothing stocky or bulky about this tall, stooping figure, and nothing hawklike in his singularly mild eye. He looked incapable of pouncing on a clue — or indeed of saying 'Boo' to a goose. That was perhaps the secret of his success; he never did say 'Boo' to a goose, but encouraged all geese and ganders to hiss and cackle to their heart's content. He was that rare thing: a philosopher who suffers fools gladly. The only quality outstanding in his character was this, and a certain meek, patient shrewdness. Meekness more often than is supposed does inherit the earth. No criminal had ever been able to believe that a bloke with a 'dial' like that could catch anybody, and so in due time Chief-Inspector Pearson caught them all.

A constable rang the Convent bell for his Chief, and so was the first to receive the death-charge of Mother Peck's eye. Though he staggered back a pace or so, he rallied gallently with a propitiatory salute.

''Scuse me, Mum; but is this the Convent of the Innacurate Deception?'

It is possible that the officer meant 'Immaculate Conception'. Whatever he meant, this description of her religious home greatly scandalised and alienated Mother Peck.

'Certainly not!'

And she was shutting the door against further offence when the Chief Inspector shuffled forward, hat in hand. His large white cravat, stiff collar, and old-fashioned cut-away grey suit reassured Mother Peck and even soothed her.

'Excuse me, Madam; but I am Chief-Inspector Pearson, of Scotland Yard. Have I perhaps the honour of addressing the Lady Abbess?'

In all the books he had read on the subject a Nunnery always had a Lady Abbess, but his pathetic ignorance made him seem almost an object of pity to Mother Peck. She uttered a short laugh, which she changed into a cough.

'*Reverend Mother*,' she emphasised, 'is

not in the habit of receiving visitors on the doorstep. I am Mother Peck. Be pleased to enter.'

The Chief Inspector did so, with an air of diffidence which Mother Peck highly approved.

'Perhaps,' he murmured, 'I might be permitted to wait upon — Reverend Mother? . . . '

Though Mother Peck was beginning to think well of this gentle-faced policeman, she thought even better of the dignity of Reverend Mother and the Convent generally. Her tone in replying was highly contingent.

'I will go and inquire what Reverend Mother's engagements are. Be pleased to take a seat.'

She indicated a bench of penitential hardness, and bustled importantly away on her errand.

Unlike the Detective-Sergeant and Dr. Goodall, the Chief-Inspector did not at all resent the treatment accorded him. He settled down contentedly to endure his vigil, and only wondered why none of the police already in the house was on the spot to receive him. How was he to know that Detective-Sergeant Osbert, being caught loitering near the lodge by Mother Peck, had been by her immured in a parlour together with an ancient aspidistra and a large portrait of Pope Pius X in the act of bestowing the Apostolic blessing? There at this moment, reduced to very low spirits by solitary confinement, he was gloomily perusing a C.T.S. tract entitled *How I Came Home*, by Lady Herbert.

'Whatever will the Inspector think!' poor Osbert was groaning to himself.

But it was characteristic of Chief-Inspector Pearson that he was leniently supposing that something very like what had happened, had happened.

'Reverend Mother is at liberty. Be pleased to walk this way.'

The voice was that of Mother Peck, and the Inspector rose to follow her, marvelling within himself that so small a woman could contrive to be so formidable and consequential.

Down the main cloister he was led by Mother Peck to a large door of ecclesiastical design cutting off the school. There were shrines of various kinds to right and left, and considerable mural painting. Outside a large folding doorway the Inspector was told to mark time while Mother Peck satisfied herself that Reverend Mother really *had* meant *now*.

Inspector Pearson remained quite passive throughout: when told to move, he moved; when told to stop, he stopped. He realized that he was up against Principalities and Powers.

It appeared that Reverend Mother definitely had meant *now*. The folding door was opened by Mother Peck, and the Inspector found himself in a large and handsome Georgian parlour with many long windows. He stood on the threshold blinking because of the strong light which poured in at these; and because, owing to the multiplication of Victorian oddments and portraits of ecclesiastics, it was impossible to be quite sure just whereabouts Reverend Mother might be.

'The police gentleman, Reverend Mother.'

So said Mother Peck, and retired bowing.

Little genial as he had found Mother Peck, the Inspector felt rather friendless on her departure; but, a cautious man by nature, he continued to stand just where he was until it should please Reverend Mother to reveal herself.

His policy was justified; almost immediately there was a movement in a window-bay; a habit drew itself upright, and the Inspector had the impression that his measure was being rapidly — and no doubt accurately — taken by a pair of bright and even pretty hazel eyes set in the pale face of a negligibly slight but somehow imposing and forceful figure of a woman.

4

REVEREND MOTHER

This little ruse of invisibility was a favourite one of Reverend Mother's, and it answered her purposes well. Upon the children it wrought powerfully, keeping them in a state of wholesome doubt as to whether Reverend Mother were really altogether of this world. The Inspector, who practised his own little ruses at the Yard, thought Reverend Mother's an excellent one.

He had, however, not the least idea how he ought to greet the Superior — whether to bow, genuflect or shake hands; but Reverend Mother put an end to his doubts by shaking him warmly by the hand.

'Good evening, Mr. Chief Inspector. How very obliging of you to give this misfortune of ours your attention.'

Policemen do not as a rule bow; they

have not the figures for it. But the Inspector bowed very low over the hand which Reverend Mother gave him.

He noted with interest that whereas he himself was installed in the most comfortable chair in the room, Reverend Mother sat bolt upright on a hard one. He had the sense to realize that this was no accident but a part of the unobtrusive but always present asceticism of these women's lives. He recalled what William James has written about the importance of the ascetic spirit as an example to a lax and lounging world.

On her side Reverend Mother was forming a very favourable impression of the Inspector. Like most nuns she was romantic on just one point, and had soon decided that he had a saintly contemplative look which she could very well imagine peering forth from the white hood of a Carthusian, those unbending sons of St. Bruno's stern reform. The more Reverend Mother thought of the Inspector along these lines the better she liked him.

She was saying:

'You must let me know all I can do to help you. I entirely realize the appalling difficulties. Even to know the names of us all . . . and then our characters . . . and the intricate little politics among us . . . '

She laughed at the Inspector's raised and deprecatory brows.

'Oh dear, yes; I assure you. When was there ever a community of women without its politics — intrigues, if you like? Do let me warn you, Mr. Chief Inspector: do not suppose that we are saints here because we base our lives on religion. We suffer here, God help us, from all the faults and failings to be found in the world outside. There is rancour and ill-will in a Convent as outside. Some of us have bad tempers. I myself have a shocking temper.'

She smiled her hazel smile, and proceeded.

'Many of us are queer, crotchety characters, and we get on one another's nerves. I know little of criminal investigation — '

She spoke as if this were a defect in her education.

'But, running a school, one learns a little in a small way. I take it we are all under suspicion until this matter is cleared up?'

It made the Inspector uncomfortable to have to admit this fact.

'Theoretically,' he murmured. 'But in practice suspicion soon narrows down.'

He coughed, and went on rather nervously.

'I admit to one little perplexity . . . '

'I am surprised it is only one. Can I do anything about it?'

Again the Inspector coughed, and closely observed his neatly spatted shoe.

'It is a matter — in itself — ah — trifling. I have the greatest diffidence in mentioning it. It is in fact the — er — *bonnet* which forms part of your — ah — most charming and becoming . . . in fact, I cannot tell one lady from another . . . '

He looked so much like a deeply troubled sheep as he put this delicate point that Reverend Mother could hardly keep from laughing.

Her answer however was deeply sympathetic.

'They *do* of course come off. But I think the Community would hardly survive the experience of a bonnetless parade. Most of them would prefer to be hanged outright. Besides, I doubt if it would help you much; the bonnet is definitely part of a nun. Without them we all look like nothing on earth.'

The Inspector was aware that it lay outside the scope of his official capacity to pay compliments to ladies of religion, so he contented himself with a dissentient movement of the legs. Inwardly he was consumed with a desire to know Reverend Mother's age. It seemed he must know it or die forever unappeased. But the age of a nun is a mystery greater than the Sphinx, and, detective though he was, he could make nothing of the face opposite with its clear skin, its small regular features, and that Protean depth of hazel eye.

Reverend Mother was proceeding:

'You must get to know some of the children. Every girl is a natural detective; nothing escapes her. If one crimp of my bonnet were to be out of place at Mass, the whole school would have commented by noon. There is not a foible in the Community which has not been told in Gath and published in the streets of Askalon.'

She ran on in that clear, sweet and yet aloof voice of hers which more and more enchanted the Inspector.

'I hope you have no masculine illusions about girls? You don't think them angels? Protestant girls may be angels, but ours are very far from it. We have children from countries where stabbing is a ladylike — and I believe a very necessary — social accomplishment. You may smile, but if poor dear Madame Sliema had made an enemy of Inez Escapado or Grazia Bombado, I could not possibly have answered for the results.'

The Inspector produced a notebook and pen. His handwriting was that of a real sleuth; it was incredibly rapid, totally illegible except to himself, and looked as if a pair of performing fleas had been taught to waltz.

His voice dropped to the tone of a consultant beginning, after some general remarks about the weather, to get down to symptoms.

'Was the deceased lady — ah — apt to make enemies?'

Reverend Mother made an eloquent gesture of the hands.

'Apt! It was her hobby! Practice had made perfect. She had quarrelled with everybody in the house, including myself. I hate to speak evil of the poor woman, but there it was.'

The Inspector made a note, and proceeded.

'I believe she was a wealthy woman? Do you know of anybody interested in the reversion of her property?'

He received a mocking hazel glance.

'Certainly I do. Unless she altered her Will, I myself was the interested party — at least, as representing this Community . . . '

The fleas waltzed.

'No one else, to your knowledge?'

Reverend Mother considered.

'She had a son — the Baron Sliema. I

always urged his being properly remembered, for the property was in the main his father's. She had, of course, quarrelled bitterly with the unfortunate young man . . . '

'Do you know where the Baron Sliema is?'

'I am afraid not. Not in England; in Spain, I have heard. Mrs. Moss would perhaps know; she was the child's foster-mother. Poor soul, she had been with old Madame for thirty years. What a martyrdom! . . . '

The Inspector was definitely inspecting now, and his fleas were waltzing finely.

'This Mrs. Moss, now? Could she have had any motive — on behalf of her foster-child?'

Reverend Mother ever so slightly shrugged.

'I should doubt if Mrs. Moss were much in Madame's confidence. She is very feeble and a chronic invalid — suffering from her heart. I believe, too, that she has what you gentlemen call an 'alibi' for the occasion. She left the chapel feeling very poorly long before Benediction was over, and Mother Peck attended to her in the garden.'

Reverend Mother hesitated, and then went on.

'It seems difficult to work out . . . such a motive, I mean. Then of course there is Venetia — Venetia Gozo — a young Maltese girl — a lay-teacher here at present . . . She was old Madame's ward . . . '

The Inspector looked very much interested indeed.

But Reverend Mother dashed him by her next remark.

'Venetia is young and strong, but she could have had no financial motive. Old Madame disliked the poor girl, of course, and had left her a mere pittance. Besides, she was right away at the other side of the altar . . . Dear me, how very unpleasant all this suspecting business is!'

The Inspector was now thoroughly warmed up and hot to be on the trail.

'I wonder,' he said, 'if I might have a look at the *locus* and observe for myself the — ah — respectivity of . . . ?'

'But of course, Mr. Chief Inspector.'

Reverend Mother rose, and the Inspector was about to follow her, when there came a light tap at the great door, and, upon permission, a small girl appeared of so rare a degree of exotic beauty that the Inspector was reminded of Gauguin. The rather dowdy uniform frock of a schoolgirl sat absurdly on this little queen of the southern seas.

'Yes, Inez . . . ?'

The child stood to rigid attention and delivered herself of a message.

'Please, Reverend Muzzer, but Muzzer Peck she say de Señor in 17 parlour 'e make de revoluccion an' refuse longer to be entertain wiz de good writings.'

At sight of the Inspector the child blushed and made a deep curtsey.

Reverend Mother smiled.

'Come in, Inez, and tell me who is this Señor who makes the revolution in No. 17!'

'Pardon, Reverend Muzzer; but Muzzer Peck she does not tell me. Only she say a Señor of much indignation.'

The Inspector beamed sentimentally

upon the exquisite Inez. He did not know if she was an angel, but he hoped there were others like her playing in the Elysian Fields.

'I think I can clear this up, Reverend Mother,' he said. 'The revolutionary person is probably Detective-Sergeant Osbert, of the Force. I rather wondered why he did not meet me at the door.'

Reverend Mother's face expressed the warmest satisfaction at one mystery the less.

'That is certainly who it must be. I expect he *was* waiting for you, and Mother Peck tidied him into a parlour. Poor man, I do hope she let him smoke.'

But the Inspector had no hope.

Reverend Mother took Inez by the hand, and, with one of those mocking hazel glances at the Inspector, said:

'If you can spare a moment, Mr. Chief Inspector, I think it really would interest you to hear about the revolution in Inez' country, Anaconda, and about how her father became the Hazh Bazh.'

'Inez glowed with delight, and, striking a pretty pose, was about to begin, when the Inspector whispered desperately aside to Reverend Mother:

'Excuse me. My stupidity, I am sure. But *what* did the little girl's father become?'

Reverend Mother waved a spacious hand.

'It's Anacondan for — their head man, don't you know? . . . Mussolini . . . that sort of thing. Now, Inez . . . '

The child resumed.

'It is de Revoluccion, Señor. Dere is big-gunning and bombing — great deal of noise. De ol' Hazh Bazh 'e come out wiz 'iz sword an' cock-'at and is making de speech, but my fazzer 'e shoot wiz 'iz revolver into de front of de Hazh Bazh. Den all de oder Señores they also shoot into de Hazh Bazh and stick deir knifes into 'im — so e' iz dead, an' dey clean him away. So den my fazzer iz de Hazh Bazh.'

'Dear me, dear me!' was all the horrified Inspector could find to say. He was aghast at the recital.

But Reverend Mother seemed to take an impish pleasure in the domestic politics of Anaconda.

'And did the other Señores agree, Inez?'

'Oh no, Reverend Muzzer. All de Señores wish to be de Hazh Bazh hisself. But when dey see de machine-gun which my fazzer point at dem, den dey agree.'

'Quite,' said Reverend Mother.

As she spoke she bared the child's arm to the elbow and compelled the squeamish Inspector to take note of a livid cicatrice in the tender flesh from the wrist upwards.

'Tell the gentleman how you got this, Inez.'

The child immediately resumed.

'It is de night of de Revoluccion. We are in de nursery, my bruzzers and sisters an' de little baby and I. Some of de Señores dey wish to make my fazzer very sorry, so dey come to kill all us who are his little children.'

The Inspector shuddered convulsively.

'So we little children when we 'ear de Señores hiding in de hacienda, we also get ready our revolvers and daggers. We obey de commands of my bruzzer

Jacquimo — 'e is very clever boy. We pile up all de nursery chairs and tables and make de *barricado*, and Jacquimo 'e dispose over de door so that a bomb fall down on de Señores when dey come in to kill us. We are careful to put de little baby b'ind de barricade.'

The Inspector groaned.

'Is this possible!'

But Reverend Mother continued to smile with a kind of radiant impishness.

'Yes, Inez?'

'De Señores dey do not expect de bomb of Jacquimo and are very discontented when it fall down on zem. But some are still alive, and dey come in and see de barricade. Dey fire at us, but we are behind de barricade. De Señores have no barricade, so Jacquimo kill zem wiz 'iz automatic-pistol which our grandma give 'im at Christmas.'

'A delightful touch!' Reverend Mother whispered aside.

Inez proceeded.

'But one of de Señores 'e arrive at de barricade and 'e stick me wiz i' knife — like that . . . '

She glanced indifferently at the frightful scar.

'But it only cut me a little, and den I stick de Señor in de t'roat. De Señores is all dead now, so Jacquimo 'e tie up my cut in de little baby's frock, an' we take de little baby, an' all go downstairs to play games. We must not go into de hacienda, for now dey are shooting with machine-guns all across. Me, I swoon sometimes because of de cut, but Jacquimo throw water out of a bucket over me. Den, soon after, my fazzer de Hazh Bazh come 'ome with my muzzer and grandma and ever so many solderos and a tank, and two of my aunties, and so we are all safe at last.'

The Inspector had sat down again, and now lay cataleptically in his chair. So this was a Convent school!

Reverend Mother however kissed the blood-stained daughter of the reigning Hazh Bazh, and cast a mischievous glance at the prostrate Inspector.

'Very well told, Inez. I should like to meet your brother Jacquimo.'

She went to a cupboard and produced what was obviously a box of chocolates

— and of no mean size.

'Now I know I can trust you to share these with all the rest of the class? Now run away, dear, and God bless you.'

With an adorable smile, and a profound curtsey distributed between Reverend Mother and the Inspector, Inez took the gift and vanished.

After a short interval of silence the Inspector drew his breath and spoke.

'The most amazing tale I ever heard. We have nothing like it at the Yard . . . '

Reverend Mother glittered at him.

'We have others almost as good. I thought you might like a practical example. When Inez first came to us she would have thought no more of stabbing than of washing her face. Indeed she would have thought considerably less.'

The Inspector regarded her much as one might a lion-tamer who has just pulled a lively young lioness by the tail. The moral of Reverend Mother's example was not lost on him.

'How did you bring about the change for the better?'

Reverend Mother answered in an offhand voice, for she knew that what she was going to say would seem strange and fantastic to the Inspector.

'Oh — by prayer . . . '

She went on at once.

'By prayer, and patience, and a sense of humour. We felt that God had played a trick on us by sending a little panther to be trained for His purposes. The idea of a lot of well-meaning old hens trying to tame a little panther is definitely funny, you must admit. I never see the child creeping along the corridors at night — with all the instincts of a wild animal still alert in her — without thinking of those lines of Blake:

Tyger, tyger, burning bright
In the forests of the night . . .

She is a relief, God bless her, after the 'Mary had a little lamb' type.'

The Inspector was muttering to himself.

'It all makes me a little ashamed to have allowed myself to remain in such ignorance. The idea current in the world — '

He broke off rather awkwardly, but Reverend Mother encouraged him with a nod and a smile.

'The idea current in the world — I confess, shared by myself until today — is that nuns are disappointed people; misfits, so to speak; emotional failures, shirking life and its problems . . . '

Reverend Mother spoke very softly.

'And now?'

The Inspector sprang to his feet and answered with energy.

'I find them — more in the nature of — Big Game hunters . . . '

He got no further, for Reverend Mother had positively clapped her hands. Her face was alive with pleasure.

'That is a delightful compliment, Mr. Chief Inspector. It puts heart into us. In return I will take you straight to the scene of your investigations — and I will rescue your subordinate from his enforced instruction in the Catholic Faith.'

5

DOCTORS (FOR ONCE)
DO NOT DISAGREE

Superiors are supposed to depute as much of their work as they can, but it was characteristic of Reverend Mother of Harrington that she could seldom depute a job which had captured her interest. It was under her personal escort that the Inspector now visited what he technically called the *locus* and cast an eye over its respectives.

The chapel of St. Joseph was on the left or Gospel side of the main altar; it was entered from the main cloister by a heavy door, and had another door leading into the main body of the chapel.

Reverend Mother pointed out that these two doors provided a thorough-fare out of chapel for visitors and nuns who had business in the direction of lodge and guest-house, but it was not used by the children.

As nobody passing out that way after Benediction had noticed anything amiss with the old Baroness, it seemed reasonably certain that she was not stabbed until some minutes after the general exodus was over. Either somebody had been waiting with the intent, or a favourable chance had been seized. The Inspector, for no reason he could have given, inclined to the latter theory.

On coming out of the chapel into the cloister, they were joined by Detective-Sergeant Osbert newly released from gaol. It was obvious that the story of his woes was trembling on his lips, but owing to the presence of Reverend Mother it continued to tremble there.

'Ah, Osbert,' said the Inspector.

And, beyond presenting the detective to Reverend Mother, that was all he said.

They all three turned right, towards the guest-house, and, skirting the lodge, soon came to the apartments recently occupied by the murdered woman.

It was but a small, plain room to have housed so much wealth, but upon examination in detail it was found to contain every creature-comfort an old woman can want.

'Of course *we* didn't furnish it,' Reverend Mother said.

Osbert was throwing open cupboards and revealing large stacks of correspondence and other literary matter.

But the Inspector had paused on the threshold of the room, and was standing there with cocked head and closed eyes, as if trying hard to remember something.

Reverend Mother watched with the deepest interest and some suppressed amusement. So this was a sleuth!

The Inspector was soon contented; he handled but few articles in the room. It was observed by Reverend Mother however that such articles as he did handle were chiefly textile, and that he passed them hurriedly and furtively under his nose.

The door was locked, and they went downstairs into the cloister again.

No sooner did Mother Peck behold the police gentlemen in the company of Reverend Mother and being by her inducted into the Priests' parlour and made free of all its amenities, than she began to take a higher view of their characters. She was further reconciled by being introduced with the words:

'This is our invaluable Mother Peck, gentlemen. I really do not know what we should do without her.'

The Inspector as usual took immense pains with his old-fashioned bow, but the Detective-Sergeant could not so soon forget his injuries.

Reverend Mother went on, taking Mother Peck affectionately by the arm.

'These gentlemen are here to help us, Mother, and so I am sure we shall do everything in our power to help them. These rooms will be their headquarters, and *all* the other parlours must be put at their disposal.'

Mother Peck opened her deeply sea-green eyes wide at this. Not even the Archbishop had ever had *all* the parlours!

Reverend Mother continued:

'You, dear Mother, with your admirable sense of organisation, will be able to help in many ways; and Sister Carmela will attend to their comfort . . . '

She added:

'Which reminds me. Mr. Inspector, while you have your conference, do allow me to send for wine and biscuits. You have had nothing since you crossed our threshold.'

The Inspector was of opinion that work is best done without wine; he merely murmured politely. But the Detective-Sergeant was thanking Reverend Mother almost with tears in his eyes.

Reverend Mother waited to see the arrival of Sister Carmela with decanters of wine and whisky and various savoury sundries, and then wished good night, being much obstructed in her departure by the extreme politeness of the Inspector.

Sister Carmela was a round-faced Maltese lay-sister with the blackest of eyes and brows, an irresistible smile, and all the physical strength and charming alacrity of her good-natured race.

The Detective-Sergeant made no secret of his admiration either of the Convent Hebe or her cups.

'This is something like!' he pronounced of the preparations. 'Do themselves well, these nuns . . . '

The Inspector was standing on the hearthrug, lost in thought; but he fired round at this.

'You mean perhaps, they do their guests well . . . '

'Right, Chief. Whatever you say. What's yours?'

But by one of those mysteries perhaps never to be satisfactorily cleared up in this world, the arrival of the decanters was almost coincidental with that of the doctors, who now came in with all that buoyancy and heartiness which autopsy imparts to truly professional spirits.

Said Dr. Goodall, as he noisily pulled a chair to the table:

'Betted these lads were boozing. Eh, Flower?'

And his colleague appeared to have had the same suspicion.

All glasses were soon brimming, and the medical officers made their report. They brought with them, very carefully disposed, the weapon which had done the deed. It was no curious stiletto of Milan steel but a surpassingly homely pruning-knife forming part of the general horticultural equipment of Mr. Turtle, the Convent's handyman.

'Home-grown enough, eh?' said Dr. Goodall, adding more whisky to his glass. 'Not much Caesar Borgia about *that*!'

The handle was tied round and round with string. When all the others were absorbed in the absorption of drink, the Inspector repeated his mysterious performance of the bedroom and passed this haft closely under his nose.

He then threw back his head, as one savouring fine cognac.

Observing the blade, the Inspector asked:

'Was it a deep stab?'

Both doctors answered at once.

'No. Hardly did more than perforate . . . And you should have seen the stays the old girl had on! More like plate armour. Shock was really what bumped her off . . . '

Dr. Goodall added, with a shake of the head:

'Clumsy work, if you ask me. Tip and run. Just what you would expect of one of these nuns with no previous experience.'

The Inspector let this pass. He interrogated Dr. Goodall.

'Not a dead stab, you say? Could it have been — do you think — the work of a child?'

Dr. Goodall filled his glass.

'Depends on age, development and ferocity of child. Not impossible, however. Eh, Flower?'

Dr. Flower also filled up, and considered.

'Doubt if young child could have got through those stays. Doubt it.'

'What is a *young* child?' inquired the Inspector.

Both doctors refused to commit themselves.

The Inspector persisted:

'Is — twelve — a young child?'

Again both experts answered at once.

'Depends. Might be — might not be, so very. No saying without examining child.'

The Inspector went on patiently.

'I want a definite answer to this. Taking

children by and large . . . such a blow as you describe, would it be wholly beyond their power at twelve — allowing for the stays?'

Dr. Flower made answer:

'My daughter Constance is exactly that age — a fine, well-developed child; plays hockey and all that. I am confident she could have produced the effects.'

He added, with a fond paternal smile;

'Only, I think Connie would have got further in.'

'The answer to my question is Yes, then?' said the Inspector.

'By and large? Oh, undoubtedly.'

The Inspector repeated himself, speaking slowly and deliberately, knowing what frivolous creatures doctors sometimes are.

'You are able to assure me that the injuries inflicted would not be wholly beyond the power of a child of twelve — taking children by and large?'

He had provided the doctors with just the saving gag their caution required. They answered severally.

'By and large. Without a doubt . . . '

'Unquestionably. By and large . . . '

It was at this point that the Inspector helped himself to a mild whisky and soda and a cheese straw.

Dr. Goodall rallied him:

'You don't drink, Inspector. Strong drink is raging, eh?'

The Inspector added soda — in such quantity that the Detective-Sergeant regarded him with pity as a man good and worthy, no doubt, and perhaps clever, but without virility.

The Inspector answered the doctor:

'I find it impairs my sense of — smell,' he said.

6

HARDLY CONCEIVABLE, BUT CERTAIN 'RIBBONS' ARE LESS THAN PERFECT, AND SEE GHOSTS FOR THEIR PAINS

The sleeping arrangements at Harrington School consist of large, airy dormitories divided on either side of a central aisle into pleasant cubicles. A nun, so placed as to be able to look down the aisle at will, presides over each dormitory and has to acquire as best she can the technique of Chaucer's 'smalë fowlës' which 'slepen al the nicht with open eeyë'.

Some senior girls however, those in the Upper Fifth and Sixth Forms, enjoy small rooms of their own, where they not only sleep at night but may retire during the day at suitable times for private study; and it was this privilege together with the excitement and disorganisation naturally ensuing on the events of the day, which enabled a number of young ladies attired in pyjamas and dressing-gowns to meet that evening for gossip and contraband chocolates in the room of Miss Verity Goodchild.

The breach of regulations was rendered more scandalous by the presence of a number of 'Ribbons' — that is, prefects, charged with the keeping of the strictest letter of the law.

It is only fair to say that the Ribbons had felt some scruples, but were in the end overruled by Miss Goodchild, who remarked:

'Oh come on. We don't kill a pig every day.'

Miss Goodchild was not a Ribbon.

Prudence Rockingham was shocked.

'Oh Verity, what a way to put it! Killing a pig . . . '

But Verity was unabashed.

'It's only your horrid mind that makes you think I meant *her*. What the phrase means, as you perfectly well know, is that this is a special occasion.'

In the end Miss Rockingham attended

the pow-wow, her Ribbon notwithstanding. Gossip and chocolates were not to be withstood considering the events of the day, and, as an extra attraction, right over the way from these bedrooms was the Guests' Wing with one large window brightly lit where it was known the sleuths were exchanging clues.

Others present on this social occasion were (Ribbons) Miss Torquilla Rohays and Miss Alauda Gale, and (non-Ribbons) Miss Philomene Watts and Miss Jamette Kestrel.

In order to add to the romance and general sleuthiness of the occasion, and also as a not unnecessary precaution, Miss Jamette was stationed near the door as sentry in case the 'Peaglums' should try on her 'Assyrian descending' stunt.

But as Miss Goodchild remarked:

'Not that anybody is likely to be on the prowl. All too scared of sleuths and ghosts.'

The slender Philomene wriggled.

'Oh, Verity, I do wish you wouldn't . . . '

'What have I done now . . . ?'

'Talking about ghosts. I don't like it. There might be, you know . . . '

Verity had stronger nerves. Indeed, she was generally remarkable for her 'nerve'.

'Fiddlesticks! Besides, haven't we got our Ribbons with us? . . . '

Miss Alauda took up the challenge:

'You seem to have got over your shock very nicely, Verity,' she remarked.

Verity tossed her head.

'I'm tough . . . '

All the same she shuddered a bit as she added:

'I didn't howl much. It was only — a bit awful — the way the old thing had sort of slumped over . . . '

There was a squeal from Philomene.

'Verity, don't. I shall never sleep. You know how badly I sleep . . . '

Torquilla, captain of hockey and senior Ribbon present, took up the running.

'The question is, who did it? Anybody any ideas?'

She circulated the chocolates, and looked inquiringly from face to face.

'Verity, what do you think?'

The reply was instant, though slightly

impeded by a caramel chocolate.

'Not a doubt about it. Pecky did it. Not her fault . . . congenital: probably dropped in infancy. She won't be hanged, but only shut up during His Majesty's pleasure. *And if I were His Majesty . . .* '

She did not finish owing to the caramel; but everybody understood and sympathised.

Jamette, from her post at the door, uttered a scoffing sound.

'Pooh! As if Pecky would ever leave the lodge — even to commit a much-needed and long-overdue murder . . . '

There were squeals of laughter, and Torquilla said:

'Yes, that lets off Pecky, I'm afraid. I tell you what: Turtle did it — or 'Mock' Turtle!'

Turtle, it may be said, was the Convent's outdoor factotum, and 'Mock' Turtle (so called by the school) was his excellent and respectable son.

But Verity would not hear of it.

'Of all the nonsense! Turtle, indeed! Who ever heard of good old Turtle in chapel! As for Mock, he couldn't swat a fly . . . He's always thinking how like St. Aloysius he is . . . '

Jamette remarked from the door:

'Excuse me, ladies; but I hear a loud noise uncommonly like the 'Peaglums' being very quiet. It might be as well — until the hideous shadow passes by — if Verity got into her blameless bed while the rest of us hide our lights under the nearest bushel . . . '

The suggestion was taken. The visitors took cover at the foot of the bed and under it, while Verity, assuming an expression of almost maudlin innocence, hopped in between the sheets.

There was no light in the room except for a pale young moon of May.

The door was gently opened, and the head of Mother Peagle put round it.

'Not asleep, Verity, dear? . . . '

'Not — quite, Mother . . . '

'Not feeling nervous or upset? Remember, the blessed Saints and Angels have us in their keeping.'

'Yes indeed, Mother.'

'If you hear any unusual sounds, it will be the police. Have no uneasiness; I shall be close at hand.'

This was exactly what Verity had wanted to know; her face was almost dewy with child-like reassuredness when Mother Peagle kissed it affectionately.

The door was softly closed again, and after a discreet interval the Witches' Sabbath re-assembled.

They all agreed about Mother Peagle:

'Sweet thing! How she does always give herself away! She's really a saint! My idea of a perfect lady! Just the sort of person to bring up girls . . . '

But the white-faced Philomene was in a trance at the window.

'Whatever is the matter, Phil? . . . '

'Oh, *look!* Oh, be *quick* . . . '

It was dark in the garden, but the moon was shedding a little eerie light among the evergreens.

In this scant and doubtful light a black figure crept gropingly — a bent figure, the figure of a nun . . .

Or was it the figure of a nun? . . .

With parted lips and pringling spines, the watchers could only gaze . . .

The figure vanished in among the

thicker evergreens — out of sight . . .

It had taken a path which all well knew — leading to the cemetery . . .

Torquilla, hockey captain and senior Ribbon, found her voice at last:

'Hush, you little fool,' she said.

For the white-faced Philomene was shaking with sobs.

7

VERITY IS KIND TO WHAT, AFTER ALL, ARE HER FELLOW CREATURES, AND IS REWARDED WITH A CLUE

Verity awoke to such a morning of sunshine and bird-song as tempted her to get up even earlier than necessary and go out into the grounds.

This was not against the rules of the school. Indeed, it was accounted an act of grace; and Mother Peagle had often said that whoever took a meditative stroll before Mass invited a special blessing.

Verity hoped she would get the special blessing, but it is doubtful if her meditations were the right sort. Her active mind ran on the mysterious figure of the night before, and she had brought with her a large magnifying glass in the hope of being able to do a little private sleuthing. She believed in dressing for her parts.

Except for the birds, and more especially a charm of goldfinches twittering sociably on the wing, Verity had — or thought she had — the bright morning world all to herself, and she followed the track of the apparition as far as she could remember it, frequently stooping low down or even going on hands and knees to use her glass. But the earth was dry, and all she got was a close-up view of innumerable little beetles all in a state of great commotion about some totalitarian excitement in the beetle world. Verity was not interested, and was rising from what struck her too late as an inelegant pose when she found herself the cynosure of the eyes of several young men perched astride upon the high brick wall.

Young men are not encouraged at a Convent school, and these must have trespassed to get where they were. Though as a rule extremely partial to the species, just now Verity was annoyed with the young men for surprising her. She tipped up her nose in disdain, and was walking haughtily away when one of them spoke to her.

'Oh, please, Miss, if you're only half as nice as you look, I'm sure you'll give us poor fellows a help-out.'

Much in this speech strongly appealed to Verity, and the voice was a pleasant one; a glance at the speaker showed him as a comely youth. But Verity was not going to relent too soon. With a further elevation of the nose she replied in freezing tones:

'I should think your best way out is the way you came in. And you had better be quick about it, for the gardener will be about soon, and he hates trespassers.'

At this point, however, she dropped the tone of virtuous reproof and asked with ardent interest:

'Who are you, anyhow?'

They all replied in chorus:

'We're the Press . . . '

'The *what?* . . . '

The first young man informed her.

'The newspapers, you know. I'm the *Daily Peephole*. You must know the *Peephole?* . . . '

Verity's eyes danced. Didn't she just know the *Peephole* — in the holidays, of course!

'And what are you all doing on that wall?' she asked.

It was the *Periscope* who answered this time. Though not so handsome as the *Peephole*, he had an arresting shock of coal-black hair and looked delightfully wicked.

'Well, there's been a murder — of all places, in a nunnery. We want a story. We've been to the door and had a statement from one of the policemen, but that's no earthly use to our readers. We want a *story*. You know what I mean?'

Verity did indeed know! And so she assured the amiably diabolic *Periscope*.

She added with studied nonchalance:

'In that case it may interest you to know that I was the person who found the — the body . . . '

'*The deuce!* . . . '

As one man the Press slipped from the wall to the ground and surrounded Verity, who stood like a princess in their midst. Unconsciously no doubt she plucked a fragrant sprig of syringa to hold against her cheek. Some of the Press had cameras!

'I shall have to be quick, or the bell will ring . . . '

'Start right in,' urged the *Peephole*.

Cameras were unslung to right and left. Note-books and fountain-pens appeared from every breast-pocket.

Verity assumed the drooping pose proper to one who tells a harrowing tale. She was wondering what on earth Reverend Mother would say, and this added a touch of real pathos to her pretty pose.

Cries of admiration greeted her.

'Hold that . . . '

Verity held it tight, and a round of applause hailed the consummation to the Picture. The *Peephole* announced the wisecrack.

BEAUTIFUL CONVENT GIRL
TELLS OF SHOCKING FIND IN
CHAPEL SPECIAL INTERVIEW

He added, rubbing his hands with exultation:

'Gosh, but this *is* a scoop! Carry on, will you?'

Verity would — and did. How true it was what Mother Peagle had said, that a meditative stroll before Mass brought a special blessing!

Amid a worshipping silence, she began her story.

'I had gone down into the chapel to — to say a prayer (sympathetic murmur, and notes all round) — I had knelt down — like this ('Hold that, please!' — and short pause). It was dark, but when my eyes became accustomed to the gloom I noticed with a dreadful sinking feeling that old Madame Sliema had fallen sideways off her priedieu — my heart almost stopped (sympathetic murmur, and notes all round) — I was incapable of the slightest movement — perspiration dabbled my brow. How I did it I do not know but I tottered to the marble rail (unanimous scratch of speeding pens) — in the dim red light of the sanctuary lamps I saw life-blood welling from the huddled form on the steps — I uttered a piercing cry, and fell prostrate — like this ('Hold that, please!' . . .)

'That's all,' Verity said.

The *Peephole* had sat down on the ground, mopping his brow, exhausted with emotion.

'Gosh, and it's the goods all right! You couldn't give us just a word about the shindy among the nuns afterwards?'

But at this moment the bell for Mass began to chime.

'I must go,' Verity said.

There was general protest. The handsome *Peephole* was imploring her.

'Just a second — one solitary second! . . . '

He indicated a tree.

'Could you just stand up against that? . . . no, the blossoming one, please . . . Gosh, but that's the ticket! You ought to go on the flicks! Could you look just a bit sad and pathetic? . . . oh, topping, topping! . . . as if the old lady were your dearly beloved grandmother or something and you wished you could see her coming up the old garden path? . . . Oh, lovely! . . . '

He addressed the photographer.
'Get that, Tommy.

BEAUTIFUL CONVENT GIRL DISCOVERER OF UGLY FACTS MOURNS DEPARTED FRIEND

How's that, boys?'

Many people cut out that picture next morning!

Verity had to tear herself away with syncopated adieux, and run. But even then the *Peephole* ran after her.

He caught up with her nimble heels, panting.

'By the way — were you — looking for anything when you — so to speak — dawned upon our sight? It wasn't this, by any chance?'

He was really amazed by the effect produced on the girl by the small object he offered her.

'Oh, *thank* you! Thank you a million times! *Where* did you find it? . . . '

'Stuck on a bush, as if it had got caught — in the kitchen-garden. Looks like a bit of nun. Is it a clue?'

'It may be. I shall find out. Good-bye . . . '

'Must you really go? There isn't an earthly of ever seeing you again, I suppose? I do wish there was. My name is Johnny Guest, *Peephole* Office. Do tell me yours. Perhaps we might pick a bone and do a show in the holidays . . . '

'Oh no, I mustn't. I'd love to, but I can't. Goodbye.'

And Atalanta had flown.

The 'bit of nun' he had given her was a long, jaggedly torn strip from a nun's veil.

8

REVEREND MOTHER READS
THE RIOT ACT

Immediately after Mass that morning the entire Community and school, and even the little tribe of domestic servants, were assembled in the Great Hall to hear an announcement by Reverend Mother and the Inspector.

It really was a Great Hall; hardly even Prize-giving filled it to capacity. But this morning it was as nearly full as it was ever known to be.

In the front, facing the stage, sat the school, graded from junior to senior. Behind were the Novices in charge of their Mistress, Mother Bunting. Behind again were the Choir Nuns and Lay-sisters. Old Mrs. Moss, a picture of weak-minded tribulation, was escorted in by Mother Trevor. Scornful and aloof among the lay-teachers sat Miss Venetia Gozo.

Prominent among the ranks of the Junior School were the black hair, red lips and Gauguin complexions of Inez Escapado and Grazia Bombado, who exchanged glances of savage hate.

Just in front of the stage was a small dais and a number of chairs for the use of Reverend Mother and the notabilities. There was also a pianoforte, with Mother Frederica stationed at it, for very little is ever done at a convent school without musical honours.

Crash, crash! went Mother Frederica on the pianoforte; and the march was so catching that portly Fr. Witherstick straightened up involuntarily and stepped out like a soldier on parade. Reverend Mother took no notice of the music. The Chief Inspector was the main attraction to the school.

'That's the head sleuth! That's the Big Boy!' So ran the general whisper. Mother Peagle had to be constantly raising an admonitory finger.

The music ceased as Reverend Mother mounted the dais. Beside her, on the chairs, were the Chief Inspector; the Very

Reverend Mgr. Todhunter, representing the Archbishop; Fr. Aloysius Birchall, Rector of the Jesuit House; Fr. Witherstick, S.J., chaplain to the Convent; several police officers, and an anonymous gentleman who (had Verity but known it) attended on behalf of the Catholic Press Association charged with the censorship of news.

Reverend Mother was no speechifier, though her clear, unstressed voice carried perfectly. She spoke informally — almost, one might have said, casually.

'I have brought you all together to tell you certain things which Mr. Chief Inspector here thinks you ought to know. My words will be very few, so that it will not be necessary for the Junior School to *wriggle* or for the Senior School to *giggle*.'

She let this sink in, and proceeded:

'We are not to shirk ugly facts, or the ugly words which describe them. We must calmly and bravely face ugly facts and the ugly words which belong to them. *Murder* has been done here among us — I regret to say, of all places, closely adjoining the sanctuary of our chapel. It is possible that the guilty person is here among us now.'

There was a pause, during which the children exchanged accusatory glances with their worst enemies, while the older girls blushed and looked down into their laps. Fr. Birchall loudly and menacingly blew his nose. Mgr. Todhunter twiddled elegant fingers nervously. Fr. Witherstick sat exactly as in the Confessional, one hand to his ear, as if expecting a penitent to break from the serried ranks and cast herself at his feet. The Novices drooped their snowy heads. Mother Trevor, that obvious saint, looked troubled and guilty.

Reverend Mother resumed.

'If that is so, then the plain course for that person is to own up at once. Mr. Chief Inspector desires me to say that he will deal with such a person with the utmost possible leniency. I am quite sure he will be as good as his word. Often people are not so guilty as they appear on the face of things. Children act impulsively; women get distracted and overwrought. We are not to fear punishment, but our real guilt in the sight of God. The Chief Inspector and myself will be in my parlour all morning, and if anybody has anything to say to us, or can throw any light at all upon what has happened, they can come to us there. I shall now ask Fr. Birchall to say a word to you.'

She stepped down from the dais, and Fr. Birchall heavily mounted it. He had a bleak, hard-boiled eye.

'I cannot add a word to what Reverend Mother has so excellently said . . . '

So he began, and proceeded to add many, many words in a loud, booming voice. His theme was sulphurous.

Mother Bunting was anxious for her Novices. The domestic servants were all practically sitting on Mother Trevor's knee. Even some of the children looked as if they might at any moment be sick.

Fr. Birchall sat down hard on the word 'Hell'.

Reverend Mother in an even calmer voice, if that were possible, immediately called upon the Chief Inspector.

The Inspector mounted the inadequate dais, caught his foot in the carpet, and fell off again, thus creating a very good impression. The school laughed and was delighted, and took the Inspector to its heart when, on re-mounting the dais, he was seen to look far more frightened than frightening. He swept them all his quaint, old-fashioned bow before beginning to speak in a low, rather flat voice.

'Reverend Mother has put everything so well. The straight way *is* the best way. Even the law is not all harshness and severity . . . '

Here he happened to encounter the full velvet glance of Inez Escapado, and added:

'It can temper the wind — to the shorn lamb.'

He looked vaguely at the clergy present.

'I am not a theologian — very far from it — only an old policeman; but I am sure these Reverend gentlemen would agree that there is mercy for the repentant — mercy for the repentant . . . '

He broke off, muttering some disjointed phrases which could not be heard.

'I only beg of you — if there is anyone here to whom these words apply — to come to your Reverend Mother and me. She — I — we — you . . . '

He became entirely incoherent, and sat down murmuring the word 'mercy'.

Reverend Mother rose with a gesture of dismissal.

'That is all. Except that none may leave the premises until further notice, everything will now carry on exactly as usual.'

9

DONKEY-WORK OF A SLEUTH

Quarter of an hour later the Chief Inspector sat in the parlour, with Reverend Mother upright beside him, and opposite him, quite collapsed in her chair, old Mrs. Moss.

No amount of gentleness and reassurance on the Inspector's part could persuade her to leave off crying and apply such intelligence as she had to the questions put to her, and finally Reverend Mother had to exert her authority.

'Come now, Mrs. Moss dear; pull yourself together. There is nothing to be in the least afraid of; you are only being asked to try and remember exactly what happened yesterday.'

The old woman mopped her red eyes weakly, but did appear to rally her faculties a little.

The Inspector was leaning far back in

his chair with that same puzzled look on his face which Reverend Mother had noticed before — as if he were trying to remember something. He seemed to be inhaling something. There was a bowl of pot-pourri on a table beside him, and it might of course be that.

He sat forward and produced his notebook, again begging Mrs. Moss not to be at all alarmed.

'I just want to check up, as we put it, Madam, on your movements after you left the chapel yesterday.'

Mrs. Moss moaned.

'It is all so dreadful — dreadful . . . '

'Now, you have not been hurt yet, dear,' said Reverend Mother. 'Try to pay attention to the questions.'

The Inspector was reading from his notes.

'Benediction at 5 p.m. prompt. You think you and Madame Sliema entered the chapel some few minutes before that time. You had come in from the garden. You were very tired and unwell . . . '

'Indeed I was, sir. Indeed it's the truth . . . '

'That is just what he is saying,' admonished Reverend Mother.

The Inspector resumed.

'Perhaps the incense set you going, but you felt very giddy and faint. You were obliged to leave the chapel at about 5.05. You staggered in the cloister, and Mother Peck saw you and came to your assistance. She took you out into the garden for a breath of air. She stayed a few minutes, and then went back to her duties. You were feeling better, but not well enough to return into the chapel. Instead you re-entered the Guest House at about 5.20 and went up to your bedroom. Benediction was just over, because you remember hearing the children singing their hymn. You are not sure if anybody saw you go upstairs, but you think Sister Carmela did. Sister Carmela also thinks she saw you come upstairs at about 5.20.'

He closed his notebook.

'Now, Madam; that has not been too trying, has it?'

He left the old woman some time for recovery after the strain of nodding her head to each of his statements, and then resumed.

'We have it from you that the late Madame Sliema had on various occasions expressed some fear of being stabbed?'

Mrs. Moss broke down again.

'It's true, sir — as God sees me . . . '

'That is exactly what he is saying,' said Reverend Mother.

'She had even,' suggested the Inspector, 'gone the length of taking certain precautions in her — ah — dress?'

Mrs. Moss looked horrified at this remote allusion to such a subject as stays, but inclined her head.

She was asked if she could throw any light on the reasons for this fear of Madame Sliema's, but it was mainly Reverend Mother who explained that old Madame had lived long in the hot-blooded south and engaged in politics.

'It was mostly vanity, however,' Reverend Mother told the Inspector aside. 'She loved to dramatise herself.'

There were several more questions dealing with old Madame's phobias, and then the Inspector said:

'Now, Mrs. Moss, I believe you were a witness of the Will deposited with Madame Sliema's solicitors? We shall have the terms of that Will today. Now I want to ask you this, had you any reason lately for supposing that Madame Sliema was going to alter that Will — that she had in fact actually done so?'

The old woman's face seemed almost to light up.

'Never! Oh indeed, never. I am sure she did not. Oh Reverend Mother . . . '

Reverend Mother soothed her.

'Well, well; that is all the Inspector wants to know.'

But Mrs. Moss was still protesting.

'Never, never, never . . . '

The Inspector produced his notebook again.

'I think,' he said to Reverend Mother, 'that is all I need trouble her with just now. Could I have a word with Miss Gozo?'

Reverend Mother nodded. Mrs. Moss was led away by one of the infirmary sisters; and a minute later Miss Venetia

Gozo made her appearance, looking sullen.

Reverence Mother noticed the look.

'Now, Venetia,' she admonished.

With an air of considerable impertinence the girl ignored Reverend Mother, and addressed herself to the Inspector.

'Am I entitled to be questioned in private?'

The Inspector looked troubled.

'Er — if you wish; certainly . . . '

'Then I do wish,' said Venetia; and with mocking politeness she threw open the door for Reverend Mother to go out.

When Reverend Mother had gone without seeming aware of the discourtesy so deliberately shown her, the girl sat down opposite the Inspector and gave him what he could only uneasily describe to himself as a look of real malevolence.

'You are Miss Gozo, I believe? You were the ward of the deceased lady?'

'I was.'

'May I put it? You were on good terms?'

'Yes.'

'You have acted as her secretary, I believe?'

'I have.'

'She conducted a considerable amount of correspondence, I believe?'

'She did.'

'She had lived long abroad, and had many friends and interests on the Continent?'

'Yes.'

'Now, Miss Gozo, about your late guardian's business-financial — affairs? . . . '

'I know nothing of them.'

'She was reticent about them?'

The girl shrugged her shoulders.

'Are you acquainted with the dispositions of her Will?'

'I am not.'

'You are left provided for, I assume?'

Venetia made no answer; her great dark eyes darkened and shone with no very pleasant light.

'Now, Miss Gozo, I have one very important question to ask you. Have you, recently, had any reason to suppose that your guardian was intending to alter her Will?'

'I had none.'

'Think carefully. Are you sure?'

There was a very slight pause, and then the girl said:

'I know nothing about it.'

The Inspector stooped down and fumbled in a small case he had beside him. From it he produced a number of Post Office Will Forms, many of them scribbled over in the handwriting of Madame Sliema. He offered them to the girl.

'Do not these look,' he suggested, 'as if Madame Sliema sometimes — ah — exercised her wit in the composition of imaginary Wills? May I ask you to look at them?'

Venetia did so, flushing as she read. The compositions were ribald in character, full of malice and personal allusions, and some passages were definitely disgusting.

Without a word she handed them back to the Inspector.

'You did not know of this — ah — hobby of your guardian's?' he suggested.

'I knew nothing of it.'

'So far as you know, then, the Will to be

opened and read today is the last and only valid testament of your guardian?'

'So far as I know.'

'Thank you, Miss Gozo.'

The Inspector rose from his chair and offered the girl his hand. She did not take it, or seem even to see it; with the sketch of a curtsey, and no relaxation of the dark brows, she turned on her heel and left the room.

10

CUT TO RIBBONS

On rejoining the Inspector in her parlour, Reverend Mother's faultless breeding had passed a complete Act of Oblivion over the disagreeable incident of Venetia Gozo. The Inspector's respect and admiration was enhanced by her total lack of curiosity; she never asked, or even hinted a question, though she was always ready to make a constructive reply to his.

True to their promise, both remained in the parlour: Reverend Mother seated at her desk writing, the Inspector studying his notebook. All round them the great establishment, with all its many and various activities, functioned without a sound.

But this state of perfect peace was disturbed before long by what sounded like the nervous approach of tiptoes in the corridor outside. This was followed by some whispering, scuffling and giggling at the door. There was a timid tap.

'*Entrez*,' said Reverend Mother, turning round from her writing.

And into the room there filed the whole erring company of last night's bedroom party, led by Torquilla in full regalia of Blue Ribbon and Child of Mary medal. Prudence and Alauda came next in similar investiture, and after them Verity and Jamette, the extreme rear being brought up by Philomene even whiter of face than usual.

All six curtseyed low to Reverend Mother and the Inspector, and afterwards stood in a row before Reverend Mother's table, blushing, wriggling their long legs, exchanging covert glances and presenting, to the Inspector at any rate, a charming picture of deep guilt combined with the most perfect innocence. His expression became fond and fatherly.

'Well, children?'

Reverend Mother looked them all six well over from top to toe with an eye which took in every detail of their dress and deportment, before she added:

'You have something to tell us? Torquilla, you are the eldest and the Senior Ribbon; you had better be spokesman. Are you quite sure Mother Peagle knows where you are?'

'Yes, Reverend Mother.'

Torquilla's peony complexion, which extended down her neck, made a fine contrast to her Blue Ribbon. It is but seldom that a sleuth sees such a blush, his way of life lying not where the sensibilities are still so strong.

'Very well, Torquilla; tell us what you have to say. Philomene, if you shudder so you will upset the ink; you had better sit down.'

The Inspector placed a chair under the trembling Philomene in the nick of time.

The five others continued to stand erect like British Grenadiers, trying not to fidget while one frightful delinquency after another fell from the lips of Torquilla in her best Elocution style.

'I see,' said Reverend Mother when the full story was told; and it was dreadfully plain to the suffering Inspector that she did.

Torquilla kept her head, though she had little hope of keeping her Ribbon — and added the story of the Creeping Figure seen among the evergreens, and concluded by producing from inside her handkerchief the piece of veil discovered by Verity in the garden only this morning. Concerning Verity's other exploits that morning Torquilla preserved silence.

Reverend Mother made no immediate comment; she took the piece of veil, examined it, and handed it to the Inspector.

The Inspector also examined it, contriving unseen to pass it closely under his nose in that curious way of his. The question he gently asked of Torquilla rather astonished his audience, even including Reverend Mother, though not a flicker of any such emotion showed on her face.

'I see you had this in your handkerchief, Miss — ah . . . Do you use any special scent?'

A certain relaxation of tension might have been noted. The girls exchanged glances, and ever so faintly tittered. Even

Philomene gave a little sputter of forlorn amusement. Did they use special scent? Did they use lipstick? Did they wear backless gowns in chapel?

'No, sir . . . '

The Inspector folded the jagged piece of veil and laid it carefully on the table. He then further examined the girls, who made a hopeless set of witnesses, contradicting one another flatly on almost every point, and only restrained from recrimination by the presence of Reverend Mother.

The Inspector took many notes however, and thanked them warmly when the examination was over, having a suspicion that there was something hot rather than warm awaiting them!

And there was!

Reverend Mother spoke:

'You are to be commended for bringing your evidence, but that was only your duty. In every other respect your conduct has been childish, irresponsible and, in the circumstances, heartless. You Ribbons will go straight from here to Mother Peagle, and resign your ribbons to her.

Verity, you will forfeit the privilege of your bedroom and go back to the dormitories. Jamette — Philomene . . . '

Her severe voice ran from deprived half-holidays to impositions. There was something for everybody, and more than enough for all. The Inspector, slumped miserably in his chair, inwardly groaned at the sentences.

'Yes, Reverend Mother.'

All six curtseyed deeply with perfect rhythm (except Philomene, who fell over a back leg), and were going to the door, the Ribbons taking off their ribbons, when a muffled sound of anguish burst from the Inspector.

'Excuse me; but if I might ask a favour. I realise it is gross — ah — impertinence. Might the — er — penalties be slightly revised in view of . . . ? I am sure these young ladies . . . In a general way . . . if I might beg as a favour . . . '

He blinked, and looked at Reverend Mother, murmuring:

'One is — ah — only young once. Even policemen break out at times . . . '

Reverend Mother gave him a reproving

shake of the head.

'And I wonder if this is how you treat them when they do, Mr. Chief Inspector! However, children, Mr. Chief Inspector has asked me to be lenient, and he well deserves to be obliged. If there are no marks against you for the next fortnight, I shall — on this one and entirely exceptional occasion — overlook your misconduct. Now, say thank you to Mr. Chief Inspector, and then get back to your classes as soon as ever you can.'

'Thank you, sir. Thank you, Reverend Mother.'

That beautiful rhythmic curtsey, seen hardly anywhere but in a Convent nowadays, set the Inspector thinking of flowers blowing in the breeze. He was relieved to see that this time Philomene kept her equilibrium. But his sentimental mood was called to order by Reverend Mother as soon as the door was shut.

'Little wretches! Now they will fancy themselves detectives! And it *would* be a nun they saw, of course! We shall have a new Maria Monk story getting about next. I suppose you detectives think nothing of this sort of thing, but it would get me down . . . '

'I don't believe anything would get you down,' mumbled the Inspector; and went as pink as a curate at a tea-party.

The hazel eye regarded him with amusement.

'If you mean by that, that I'm tough, I certainly am.'

She picked up the piece of veil from the table and looked it over again critically.

'What do you make of this? I suppose it *is* a clue?'

The Inspector had no sooner paid his little compliment, which was wrung from him involuntarily, than he became acutely sensible of the impropriety of his conduct, and dared not meet Reverend Mother's eye. He was silent, and Reverend Mother spoke for him.

'It is a matter easily cleared up. I will go and make inquiries. Clothes cannot get torn here without note being taken, any more than in the Army . . . '

The Inspector found his voice again.

'By all means let us identify it,' he said slowly. 'But I am already pretty clear in my — mind — that, as relating to any member of the Community, it is without value.'

On her way to the door Reverend Mother paused, and regarded the Inspector with that luminously intelligent expression which was perhaps her most attractive.

'You can say as much already? That is really very clever, and relieves my mind.'

She added, with a cordial smile:

'It is mid-morning, and I am sure you must be fainting. I shall send Sister Carmela with madeira and biscuits.'

The Inspector longed to say that Reverend Mother required a 'small spot' quite as much as he did, but he remembered in time that Reverend Mothers do not hobnob with police officers over 'small spots' in their parlours. He had to content himself with throwing his whole soul into the way he swept open the door for Reverend Mother and bowed almost double as she passed through.

'I should like, if possible,' he murmured, 'to see the *whole* veil, of which this piece formed a part.'

11

THE CHIEF INSPECTOR SHOWS HIS (PROBABLY FALSE) TEETH

Probably by that same magic which had wrought upon the doctors the night before, the advent of Sister Carmela, smiling, with the decanter, at once summoned up Detective-Sergeant Osbert, looking very sleek and pleased with himself. Osbert was a capable officer but not a man of delicate perception; auras and *nuances* were lost upon him: he strode the highly polished floor of Reverend Mother's parlour with a jaunty air of proprietorship, and he bestowed the broadest of broad winks on Sister Carmela. He had a breezy manner towards his superiors, which some said would obstruct his career.

'Well, Chief; how are stunts at your end? Any depositions, informations or confessions? . . . '

Osbert's manner was offensive to the Inspector, who answered crabbily.

'Must you speak at the top of your voice? And keep your confounded boots off that rug . . . '

It is doubtful if the confident young detective even heard the rebuke; he had produced a mass of foolscap sheets covered with hand-writing, which he shied down on Reverend Mother's table on top of the letter she had left there.

'Well, sir,' he informed his superior, 'the grass hasn't been growing under my feet, I can tell you. Combed the whole bally place with a bally comb, I have. Here's plans of St. What's-his-name's chapel with reference to all the main exits and entrances. Here's depositions, and more depositions. Not one of the ladies missing, sir. And here's the best we could make of the kids — did 'em at their lessons, taking a half dozen at a time. There's some salty little sprats among 'em, I can tell you!'

He guffawed to himself as he profusely wetted his thumb and turned over the sheets.

'I don't know how it appears to you, sir,' he added, 'but to my way of thinking there's something remarkably fishy about this Benediction they were all at. It isn't natural, like, if you ask me.'

The Inspector answered coldly.

'I see nothing — ah — fishy in it. This is a religious house, and Benediction is one of the principal devotions of the day.'

The Detective-Sergeant looked shrewd.

'All the same, Chief, it don't accord with my ideas of what's natural — all this going to church at odd times on a weekday. For everybody to be in church on a week-day looks to me uncommonly like hanky-panky. I've an idea we could shake some of 'em of that alibi if we put it across 'em, sir.'

'What did I say about your boots and that rug?' said the Inspector testily, and he removed the police-reports from Reverend Mother's table. But he pushed the decanter in Osbert's direction, and rather grumpily told him the story of the bedroom party, the creeping figure and the piece of veil.

Osbert smacked his lips over the wine

and over the recital.

'Why, Chief, that about clinches the matter. Find out who that veil belongs to, and, Benediction or no Benediction, there's your man — I mean, woman — that is, nun. You'll probably find that the old girl had some dibs — one of these nuns gets wind of it — bumps off the old girl and collars the dibs. What about that?'

'A trifle obvious,' drawled the Inspector, directing a glance of intense dislike at his subordinate's boots.

They were interrupted by the re-appearance of Reverend Mother. The Inspector immediately rose, but Osbert continued to lounge at his ease with one large boot on a dainty figured settee.

'Well, Mr. Chief Inspector, I have traced the veil. You were certainly right. It is part of one of Mother Trevor's veils!'

Reverend Mother almost laughed aloud.

Mother Trevor! Both policemen had experienced the gentle charm of this lady. But the Detective-Sergeant, after a gasp of disappointment, had recourse to the adequate supply of police stupidity.

'I don't see,' he argued, 'as its belonging to one lady or another makes any difference.'

Reverend Mother's eyes rested momentarily on the boot which rested on her settee.

'Don't you, sir? Then I am sure no one can enlighten you.'

She added, annihilating Osbert and addressing the Inspector:

'Mother Trevor is much distressed. She has tried her best but cannot remember how the veil could have got torn. If you can help her to clear the matter up, it will be a great relief to her.'

She declined the Inspector's urgent offer to wait upon Mother Trevor wherever it might be convenient, and went off herself upon the errand.

The Detective-Sergeant took the opportunity of filling up his glass again.

'It's all very well, Chief,' said he, 'but if you're going to let holiness and what not count in a shop like this, you might as well chuck in the sponge and go home. These heavenly alibis don't fit in with my idea of a case. As I was putting it to you, about this here Benediction . . . '

He was still talking when Reverend Mother came back, ushering Mother Trevor.

'Please don't let us interrupt you, sir,' said Reverend Mother. The two ladies sat down closely side by side on their upright chairs, and it was observed by the Chief Inspector that Mother Trevor's thin hands were working upon her lap. Her face was a little pinched, and she seemed to have a cold.

The Inspector's voice as he put his interrogatory was as gentle as a Father Confessor's. It annoyed the Detective-Sergeant, who thought all the signs favourable for a little brow-beating.

It was soon clear that Mother Trevor was utterly at sea. She clasped and unclasped her hands, sometimes glancing at Reverend Mother for assurance.

'I am sadly careless — but somehow I cannot remember . . . And how *could* I be out at such an hour? It is against our Rule . . . '

The Detective-Sergeant, unable any

longer to resist his instinct and training, rose to his feet and pointed a large, blunt forefinger at the shrinking Mother Trevor.

'All very well, Madam, all very well. But how do you account for this torn piece of your clothing? ... '

Mother Trevor whispered her reply in a tone of despair.

'I am — afraid I — cannot, sir ... '

The Detective-Sergeant enjoyed all the dominant sensations which a lusty young snake must feel when it really does succeed in fascinating and bewildering a bird with its eye. He proceeded with thickened and coarsened voice, keeping the blunt finger in a line with Mother Trevor's bowed head:

'You say you *cannot?* Are you sure, Madam, that you do not mean — you *will* not? Are you sure you do not mean — I have reasons for wishing *not to?* Come, come, Madam; this is no *nunnery* affair. This is a police investigation into *murder.*'

In another minute, the Detective-Sergeant told himself, they would be at the point of a 'statement under warning';

this woman was obviously on the run.

But then a rare phenomenon occurred: Chief Inspector Andrew William Pearson suddenly and violently lost his temper.

'Oh *shut* up, Osbert, you clumsy fool! This isn't a children's party. Reverend Mother will find some other time for you to try your comic policeman stunt on the younger children.'

He went on without a pause, addressing Reverend Mother and Mother Trevor.

'I beg your pardon. I have not the slightest doubt that *someone else* was wearing Mother Trevor's veil when it got damaged.'

His words seemed still further to confuse Mother Trevor, but Reverend Mother was on to their full import in a second.

'You mean — the veil was stolen? . . . '

'It would be possible, I suppose?' said the Inspector. 'It must be possible, for I am sure it was done. The figure the children saw last night — the creeping figure — was wearing a stolen veil . . . '

He added, after a pause:

'And the veil may be stolen again — or some other. I think myself it will be.'

The Detective-Sergeant mopped his brow, and gaped. All the 'comic policeman' was gone out of him; and he remembered with misgiving some professional gossip to the effect that, sheep as old Pearson looked, he could turn on short notice into a ravening beast of prey. The vision of a constable's uniform swam before his eyes.

Reverend Mother had risen, and raised Mother Trevor with her.

'Now, dear Mother,' she said, 'you see the *Inspector* perfectly understands.'

She accompanied her words with a radiant glance at the Inspector, who appreciated it from the crown of his head to the soles of his feet.

He mumbled his reply, as usual when wrought up.

'I again apologise to Mother Trevor. I am so sorry she has been exposed to this strain.'

He broke off, and added in the voice of a Regimental Sergeant-Major on parade:

'*Osbert, have you hands?*'

The discomfited Detective sprang to attention.

'I have been under that impression, sir.'

'*Then use them to open the door for these ladies.*'

Mild and clerical-looking as the Inspector was, there was the ring of steel in his voice. Reverend Mother rejoiced to hear it.

The Detective-Sergeant obeyed but with poor grace; at no time much in the habit of opening doors for ladies, he thought it the extreme of humiliation when on a case. Only Mother Trevor acknowledged his clumsy salute. Reverend Mother's acknowledgement was directed back to the Inspector, who stood simmering in a window-way.

'Thank you, Mr. Chief Inspector. Please remember, I am always at your command . . . '

The ladies passed out on their dignified way; and the Detective-Sergeant, after a glance backwards, made a bolt of it after them. He desired no more conversation with the minatory frown of the Chief Inspector.

12

TURTLE SOUP

Sitting after an excellent luncheon in the Priests' Parlour the Inspector considered things.

On a careful balance of all the evidence the time of the murder narrowed down to about three minutes — between 5.20 when the children left the chapel, and 5.23 as near as possible when Verity returned to it. All was well with Madame Sliema at 5.20, and all was over with her by 5.23. In the Inspector's belief the murderer had seized an opportunity, entered St. Joseph's by the cloister door, done the deed, and, as the Lancashire expression has it, 'made himself scarce' with all possible speed so as to set up an alibi. The crime had the look of a thing resolved upon beforehand and executed as luck served.

Apart from the general dislike in which

Madame Sliema was held, nobody seemed to have any special motive for killing her. The Inspector, in his own mind, set down the motive as certainly revenge. But revenge for what injury? Well, the terms of her Will might throw light on this point, and the Will was to be brought to the Convent that afternoon.

The girl Venetia interested the Inspector. There was certainly some as yet unknown factor there, but her rude manner under examination did not suggest guilt to the Inspector, it looked much more like complicity. It looked as if she were determined at all costs not to give something away. Well, of course she would have to give it away; whatever it was she wished to defend and protect (and that was how the Inspector described her manner to himself) time would pretty certainly show.

If Mrs. Moss had done it, then she must have got new life for the purpose, for there could be no doubt as to her feebleness and utter incapacity for decision and action. It was unlikely, to say the least of it, that after thirty years of submissive servitude she would suddenly develop resentment to the point of murder. However, in these days of psychology, nothing could be ruled out as absolutely impossible. Again there was some unknown factor; the old woman was certainly very uneasy about something. The vehemence with which she had disclaimed any knowledge or suspicion of a new Will had but served to convince the Inspector that here was a very sore spot indeed.

Beguiled by the lovely weather, the Inspector got up and strolled out into the beautiful grounds. A cricket match between pick-up sides was in progress on the field, and the Inspector stood absently watching it for some time. The game seemed to involve more hilarity than is usual with cricket. The players laughed at every stroke, and went off into fits when Torquilla, at the wicket, stepped out and swiped a boundary.

'*Oh, well played the Sleuths!*' ran the general acclamation; and, from this and other cries which came to his ears, the Inspector gathered that the match had taken the form of *Sleuths v. Nuns*, and that *Sleuths*, the popular side, was distinguishing itself.

His own appearance was greeted with loud applause, and he had to acknowledge the salute of many waved hands. The whole thing cheered him up, and he walked on wondering why he had never married and had a tribe of children.

As he strolled down towards the kitchen-garden and orchards he was mildly surprised to encounter a bandit. At any rate he encountered an elderly male person of gnarled and weather-beaten appearance who had closely studied the general get-up of banditry; he was wearing a slouch hat at a rakish angle, a khaki shirt wide open at the neck, a pair of ancient green corduroy pants, stout leather leggings and even stouter boots. A clay pipe was stuck in his mouth, and he was armed with a hoe.

Mildly surprised at the picturesque nature of all this, the Inspector was not otherwise surprised, for he guessed the bandit to be that very Mr. Turtle, the Convent's gardener, whom in fact he had come out to interview.

He was about to introduce himself when the bandit saved him the trouble.

'Excuse my freedom, sir; but be you the gent as is inquirin' into the 'orrible crime perpetrated up at the 'ouse yonder?'

The Inspector smiled and bowed.

'I am Inspector Pearson,' he said; and shook the immense hand which was thrust at him.

'Well, then, sir, breaking no bones and beating no bushes but my name is Turtle, and a word with you where there ain't no women about, it was my wish.'

'Mine too, Mr. Turtle.'

Mr. Turtle looked gratified, as a bandit might whose prisoner surrenders at once with a good grace.

'Which, sir, that bein' the flatterin' an' mutual case, to the tool-'ouse let us go, for I will not deny, that is my 'eadquarters, like, and gardening is my profession.'

'A delightful occupation, Mr. Turtle.'

Mr. Turtle spat aside, covered his large whiskery mouth with his hand, and became confidential.

'Which it would be, sir, but for women; but when you gets women, sir, as thinks they knows more about it than yourself, then it is as if the angel with the Flamin' Sword was standing at the gate.'

The Inspector tactfully turned the subject, and they arrived at the tool-house. Mr. Turtle sat in a wheelbarrow, and the Inspector on an upturned bucket.

The Inspector admired the fine gardens.

'Which it is all the work of myself and my son, Mock, sir — though why they calls him 'Mock' I do not know, for mock he never did, and I would 'a warmed him if he 'ad.'

He spat again, and added:

'But let us not prevariagate, sir, for we are men, not women, and our minds are nateral formed for seriousness.'

'By all means, Mr. Turtle.'

The Inspector knew far better than to hurry him.

'Not knowing your views, sir,' said Mr. Turtle, 'I cannot speak for 'em, but I am one as never did hold with too much church-going. It may be a disfirmity, but there it is. When the ladies says to me, 'Why don't you come to church, Turtle?' I makes no reply, but I asts myself, What would the Lord want with Turtle for ever getting under 'is eye? I ain't denying as God made me, sir, but so in a manner of speaking did I make my son Mock — with a bit of 'elp from Mrs. Turtle; but because I made my son Mock, sir, do that mean to say as I wants to see him forever underfoot and hanging round like?'

Mr. Turtle smote his palm.

'It does not, sir!'

The Inspector nodded gravely.

'I quite see your point, Mr. Turtle. You are going to tell me however that, in spite of your general principles, you did go to Benediction on the evening of the crime?'

Mr. Turtle removed his pipe from his mouth and his hat from his head, scratched the crown of the one with the stem of the other, and stared.

'Which not a breathing soul saw me, sir, nor did I let on to nobody. So how you come to know about it . . . '

The Inspector laughed.

'I only said you were going to tell me,

Mr. Turtle. All the same I noticed yesterday evening that extensive gardening had been going on in that part of the garden. Then of course the knife used was a gardening tool. Neither old Mrs. Moss nor Mother Peck mentioned seeing you in the garden, so I took the liberty of supposing that you were not there just at that time but had gone in to Benediction.'

Mr. Turtle resumed his hat and pipe, and spoke sadly.

'It was a sudden weakness, sir, as I will not deny. We are all taken inconstituent sometimes, sir . . . '

'Then, of course,' the Inspector went on, 'there was the evidence of the knife. It is a fair assumption that you were not on the spot when that knife was picked up by the murderer. Isn't it now?'

Mr. Turtle showed signs of again removing hat and pipe for a refresher. He spoke in his beard.

'A bike-rider I've been, which likewise a motor-bike, but this is going too fast for me.'

'There is nothing very much in it, Mr. Turtle. You were going to tell me all this.

The important thing is, when you went to Benediction what did you see?'

'I come in late, sir,' said Mr. Turtle, as if this were at least some extenuation of his conduct, 'and I kneels down at the back handy for gettin' out, — and I see old Madame Sly-ema, as she called herself, a-cocked up on 'er pray-do a-prayin' away fit to bust 'erself. First thing as 'appens, up jumps little Mrs. Moss, green as a gooseberry, and rushes out — as if, sir, for a basin.'

'Yes, Mr. Turtle? . . . '

'Well, sir, she looked bad, Mrs. Moss did — same as I've seen 'em when goin' to Margate by sea. I puts me 'ead round door and sees Mother Peck come clicketin' up and 'urry the patient to the open air.'

'Yes, Mr. Turtle? . . . '

'Well, sir, after that everything proceeds accordin' to specification. The ladies and the young gals they sings 'ymns, and the little lad with the smoke-box 'e' alf chokes me. And then, sir — why, it's all over, like . . . '

'Exactly. And then, Mr. Turtle? . . . '

'I come out, sir, fast as ever I could and makes for to get back to me work by way of the cloister door . . . '

'Did you see anyone?'

'Well, sir, if by that you mean did I encounter anybody, the answer is as I encountered nobody . . . '

'That is not quite answering my question, is it, Mr. Turtle? I said, did you see anyone?'

At this point a refresher became absolutely necessary for Mr. Turtle; he spat, removed hat and pipe, scratched, and wiped his brow.

'Sir,' he said, 'from a little 'un I have had 'em — my eyes is short, sir, and me glasses they was not on me nose. If I see anything, sir, it must be without prejudice and giving the benefit of the doubt . . . '

'Of course, of course. You can only tell me as nearly as you saw. What did you see?'

'I see a human form, sir, a-come quick to that there chapel door, and go in . . . '

'Can you describe the form you saw?'

Mr. Turtle answered with some reproach in his voice.

'From a little 'un, sir, as my sight is dim, and me glasses was not on me nose. What I see, sir, I see but with the tail of my eye, and 'aving no reason to suppose as games was being played . . . '

'At least you can tell me if it was a man or a woman?'

'You ain't a Catholic, sir — if I may make so bold?'

The Inspector shook his head a little impatiently.

'Does that make any difference?' he said.

'Sir, askin' your pardon, but it do. In the Catholic Church, sir, the men wear petticuts same as the women, so how is a man to tell if a human form seen with the tail of the eye is one sect or t'other?'

'At least it seemed to you to wear skirts?' the Inspector said.

'But it is from a little 'un,' said Mr. Turtle, 'as I have suffered from optical defect . . . '

The Inspector tried again.

'You didn't by any chance notice the exact time of this?'

Mr. Turtle proudly produced an enormous, old-fashioned watch from somewhere about his person.

'Which it so 'appens I did, sir, and there ain't a better watch in England. Belonged to me grandfather, sir. Feel the helf of it.'

The Inspector did so, and nearly dropped it.

'That's the weight a watch oughter be, to be a good 'un,' said its owner; 'not a goo-gaw same as these silly women is always late by.'

He added:

'Which it is always my 'abit to take note of the time, sir, whenever I am about to reshoom work, for it is but right as a man should be paid for all he done. The time, sir, was 5.22 to a tick.'

'Thank you, Mr. Turtle.'

The Inspector got up off his bucket and took a turn up and down the path.

'And when you discovered the loss of your gardening-knife, Mr. Turtle? What did you think then?'

'Sir, I didn't think nothing, for the tricks as 'as been played on me, and is constant being played, you would not as a gentleman believe.'

Mr. Turtle spat.

'Call 'em Convent young ladies,' he muttered. 'I could bite a better Convent young lady out of a piece of bread and butter.'

The Inspector drew up and suddenly sprang it upon Mr. Turtle.

'I suppose you didn't by any chance do it yourself?'

Mr. Turtle's features lit up with a broad smile.

'Wot? Bump off old Sly-ema? Well, sir, there weren't no love lost betwixt us, and if the idee and the opportunity 'ad occurred coincidental, perhaps I might have. But as it 'appens, I did not.'

'I believe you, Mr. Turtle,' said the Inspector; and they shook hands.

It took the Inspector a long time to disentangle himself from his new friend, for Mr. Turtle, finding that the Inspector was a bit of an amateur gardener, wished to introduce him personally to a large number of distinguished vegetables.

It was after a fifth and final handshake

that the Inspector made his escape, with the words:

'Thank you, thank you, Mr. Turtle. An interesting chat, and a fine exhibition. Now do let me beg of you, keep your eyes open and keep your glasses on.'

'Which I will, sir,' was Mr. Turtle's reply, cordially voiced; 'which I will. And if you, sir, should ever find the oppression of women too much for you up at 'ouse, you come down 'ere and refresh yourself with Turtle.'

13

THE WILL – BUT WHAT ABOUT THE WILE?

A sedate gentleman from the firm of Messrs. Locke, Sharpe, Truebody, Truebody & Thompson, Madame Sliema's solicitors, was waiting for the Inspector when he got back to the house.

He introduced himself by the name of Truebody-Jones, and handed over in a heavily sealed package the Last Will and Testament of the late Baroness Sliema.

Between them they broke the seals and produced the document.

'Did she make this, here in her own apartments, or at your office?' the Inspector inquired.

Mr. Truebody-Jones replied that the Will had been made by Madame the Baroness herself here on the premises.

Whereupon — but without attracting the attention of Mr. Truebody-Jones

— the Inspector passed the document under his nose.

Together they read it through, and a very proper Will it seemed in all respects to be. When all taxes, duties and charges were deducted, there would remain £100,000 to be divided equally between the Convent of Harrington (in the name of Reverend Mother) and the testator's only son, the Baron Crauford Sliema.

A small provision was made for Venetia until she became of age, when she would inherit a patrimony of £100 a year; and the Convent was asked to take over the guardianship of her.

Mrs. Moss had £200 a year, chargeable on Crauford.

Those were the main provisions.

'A highly orthodox and satisfactory document,' Mr. Truebody-Jones allowed himself to comment.

Abstractedly, but with considerable graphic power, the Inspector sketched a skeleton on the blotting-pad.

'Were you well acquainted with your late client?' he inquired of the solicitor.

Apart from business affairs Mr.

Truebody-Jones had not had the pleasure.

'We are in confidence here,' the Inspector said. 'Did you know the contents of this Will? Now that you do know, is it what you expected?'

'In the strictest confidence, Mr. Inspector, I did not — er — anticipate so equitable a disposition.'

'You had grounds for that?' suggested the Inspector, further articulating his ghastly skeleton.

'I believe,' the solicitor said, 'that the very unfortunate alienation of the deceased Baroness from her son is fairly common knowledge.'

'Do you know the cause of it?'

Mr. Truebody-Jones faintly shrugged.

'I do not, Mr. Inspector. I have heard that it is of very old standing — in fact, that the late Baroness never cared for her child.'

'So you rather expected to find the natural heir cut out, did you?'

'I was under some apprehensions, I will own, Mr. Inspector. Speaking professionally, such things are always regrettable.'

'Most,' agreed the Inspector.

He finished his skeleton.

'Now, Mr. Truebody-Jones,' he said slowly, 'can you tell me this? Had you been given any reason to suppose that Madame Sliema wished to alter the Will we have just read? It is a matter of some importance.'

The lawyer glanced at his own features in the glossy silk of the top-hat beside him.

'I am able to assist you, Mr. Inspector. Madame Sliema apprised us some days ago that she was altering her Will . . . '

'She did not actually send for you?'

'She did not, Mr. Inspector. But she was perfectly competent to draw up a valid Will without professional advice.'

His strictly impersonal professional veneer suddenly cracked a little, and he spoke with urgency.

'She may have done it. I would not put it past her. In your examination of her apartments and effects, you discovered no such instrument? . . . '

'No,' said the Inspector, rather vaguely.

'You may still do so, Mr. Inspector,'

said Mr. Truebody-Jones. 'I have known it again and again, especially with elderly women of imperious temper: a sudden splenetic outbreak . . . you understand? . . . '

'Perfectly,' said the Inspector. 'That is why I put these questions to you.

He added, speaking very deliberately:

'I am convinced that she was murdered over that altered Will.'

The human Truebody-Jones had entirely relapsed into the man of law.

'Dear me!' he said.

When Mr. Truebody-Jones had taken his leave, the Inspector sat on at the table, adding an open grave and a neat little headstone to his skeleton.

14

VERITY JOINS THE POLICE FORCE

Early the following morning there was a telephone call from the Catholic Press Association inquiring with a touch of irony if Reverend Mother's attention had been called to the current issues of the *Peephole* and the *Periscope*.

Mother Peck replied with asperity that Reverend Mother's attention had not been called; and she was proceeding to pass a few general remarks on the character of both papers when she was informed that none the less Reverend Mother would probably be interested in to-day's issues, and rung off.

The papers were sent for, and nearly proved fatal to Mother Peck, for there, broadly printed upon the front page of the *Peephole*, was a fine study of Mother Peck herself, taken at her own sacred portal, obviously in the act of repelling some undesirable person — and above, in vast black letters, was the caption:

CONVENT MYSTERY
INTERVIEW WITH LADY SUPERIOR
LADY SUPERIOR RECEIVING SPECIAL
'PEEPHOLE' REPRESENTATIVE AT
DOOR OF CELL.

This striking *coup* had been achieved by the young Pressman with the ease of perfect impudence: the *Peephole* rang the bell, and tried to sell the Convent a Hoover or some such appliance; then, while Mother Peck was in the very act of repudiation, an invisible photographer 'got' her full in the face, — and next minute, full of lively satisfaction in work well done, all the young men were rolling down the road together towards the nearest pub.

The unmaidenly posings of Verity, and the incredible nonsense she was made to say, passed — by Mother Peck at any rate — comparatively unnoticed. It was her own shocking appearance as Reverend

Mother that smote her figuratively to the ground.

A figure of pathetic dignity, reminding our representative of the beautiful but ill-fated Queen of Scots, the Lady Superior stood waiting at the door of her cell inside the sacred enclosure.

Unable at first to articulate for the sobs which caught at her throat, she pointed to a conventual chair of Gothic pattern . . .

She spoke in high praise of the *Peephole*, and of its influence for good upon our British millions . . .

So ran the interview.

Reverend Mother abhorred the vulgar publicity of today. She had not much difficulty in seeing how the reporters had tricked Mother Peck, but the portraits of Verity were too obviously deliberate poses on that young woman's part. As she sent word to Mother Peagle that Verity Goodchild be ordered instantly to the parlour, her face had that stretched look, as of fine material over a frame, which it only had when she was very angry indeed.

Miss Goodchild was one of those wise and prudent virgins who keep their lamps always trimmed. Knowing what might be in pickle for her this morning, she had been at pains to make it difficult for Mother Peagle to search her out, her object being to give Reverend Mother time for second thoughts so that haply she might be spared the sin of anger and the even greater sin of hasty action.

'Where is Verity?' cried Mother Peagle, hurrying from pillar to post, and dispatching her Ribbons far and wide to aid the search.

But Verity was nowhere to be found.

In the meantime the Inspector had arrived at the parlour on a mission of his own, and had been told the facts.

He read the 'interview' with the 'beautiful but ill-fated' Mother Peck without the twitch of a face muscle, but his habitual gravity deepened when Reverend Mother declared that this time Verity had gone too far and would have to be sent away.

He spoke gravely.

'Technically, you know, she cannot leave the Convent just now; nobody can. And do you know, Reverend Mother — '

He stroked his admirably-shaven chin.

'Do you know, I think you are being a little hard on the child?'

For answer Reverend Mother held out the picture of Verity fallen in a faint upon the ground.

'Hard!' she echoed.

The Inspector looked at the picture.

'It is only acting,' he said. 'The girl is only playing a part. A gang of these young Press toughs got hold of her and she couldn't resist their blarney. Few girls could. There is nothing — ah — in the least *improper* about these pictures.'

'There is vanity, thoughtlessness, dis-obedience and unmaidenliness in them,' declared Reverend Mother.

But then she burst out laughing.

'You know, Mr. Inspector, you are badly taken in about girls. I suppose most men are.'

'Quite likely,' agreed the Inspector. 'And yet I think that a man, precisely

133

through standing further off, may sometimes get a better view of a girl's character. His judgments, too, are more lenient . . . '

'I can hardly overlook this altogether,' Reverend Mother said.

'Why not?'

'My dear Mr. Inspector! Won't it be enough for you if I stop short at reducing this naughty child to the dormitories? . . . '

The Inspector spoke slowly.

'I am going to beg of you not even to do that.'

He began to speak quickly.

'The fact is, I want a sharp eye in one of those bedrooms overlooking the guest-house . . . '

Reverend Mother sighed.

'This police business is the ruin of discipline! And what would you have me say to this bad child when she chooses to put in an appearance? Am I to congratulate her on the undoubted beauty of the pictures?'

The Inspector bent his mind to the problem of a suitable rebuke, and looked so solemn and earnest about it that Reverend Mother relapsed into laughter.

'I am half inclined to leave you to it,' she said.

She might well laugh, for the fatherly — or at least avuncular — attitude of the Inspector had been growing from hour to hour. It now comprehended not the school only, or even the Novices and Community, but Reverend Mother herself, whom he would gravely reprove for not taking enough rest and for persisting in running her own errands. Several little lectures he had given her in his kindly, solemn way, and she had richly enjoyed both them and him. His nickname in the Community was 'Grandmother Dear', after Mrs. Molesworth's delightful story. Sister Carmela was devoted to him. Mother Peagle had several times found him playing clumsy and laborious cricket with the Junior School.

'I should be firm but gentle,' said the Inspector after prolonged deliberation. 'I should point out her error clearly . . . '

Reverend Mother assured him.

'Yes, I will do that.'

'And then,' added the Inspector, 'I should tell her to move her bed to the window and sleep with one eye open.'

Later that same day Verity confided to Torquilla and Philomene:

'I don't want to alarm you, children, but in my opinion Reverend Mother is breaking. Definitely! All this murder business has undermined her resistance. She is not what she used to be. She only told me today that I had disgraced myself — my people — the school — the Convent — the Pope — the Church — and every principle of the Catholic Religion . . . '

15

INQUEST

A Coroner's Inquest as prescribed by the laws of this country is a sordid affair, unredeemed by a single touch of the picturesque.

There is no scarlet judge, no Sword of Justice. There are no good-looking young Counsel in wigs and gowns.

There was, moreover, not the smallest chance for Miss Verity Goodchild to show off; her voice and manner in giving evidence resembled those of a mouse with a cold.

She was deeply disgusted. This drab court, this commonplace little man who was the Coroner . . . all these horrid medical particulars . . . Here was no story for Torquilla, Alauda and the rest.

Nor was Mr. Turtle, called upon to swear to the knife, any better pleased.

'Are you in the habit of leaving

dangerous cutting instruments about in a place where there are children?'

To which Mr. Turtle rejoined, with some tartness, that if a bloke couldn't put down his tool for a few minutes — in a Convent, mind you — and him only going for as long as it took a man and not a woman to say his prayers, — without having that tool picked up and introduced between the ribs of a third party, well, he, Turtle, would be blowed, and he couldn't say fairer than that.

Some spice was lent to the proceedings, however, by a long discussion of stays, and Madame Sliema's reasons for wearing such very 'valiant' ones (the term was the Coroner's). The Coroner was not without a sense of his duty to the public in such a case as this, and his knowledge of 'artificial supports' appeared to be large. A special edition of the evening papers went quickly off under headlines:

NUNNERY MURDER MYSTERY
CORONER ON STAYS

Mrs. Moss, supported into the box with

smelling-salts and brandy, was embar-
rassed almost into a swoon as she listened
to Dr. Goodall and the Coroner exchanging badinage about her late mistress's
stays.

Reverend Mother explained Madame
Sliema's status in the Convent. Mothers
Peagle and Vannes corroborated Verity's
story.

The Coroner summed up at great
length, and concluded by suggesting the
terms of the verdict.

The jury brought in the verdict, after
carefully altering all the terms.

Madame Sliema had been murdered by
a hand or hands unknown.

Verity was not impressed by the verdict;
she herself had known it all the time.
Fancy all that fuss just to establish what
everybody knew!

Torquilla and the rest flocked around,
eagerly questioning, but Verity assumed a
grown-up pose.

'Not just now, children; I am far too
tired. You have no idea of the strain of
cross-examination by a skilled barrister of
deadly purpose. Keeping your head, you

know — and never committing your-self . . . '

She retired, in a cloud of half-sceptical glory, to her bedroom.

'Verity gets all the fun,' Jamette sighed.

Philomene was seized with one of her attacks of lisps, denoting strain.

'It wath me that thaw the ghotht,' she said.

'You would!' was the crushing rejoin-der. 'And got us all half slain by Reverend Mother.'

Meanwhile, downstairs in the Priests' Parlour over a cup of tea eagerly provided by Sister Carmela, the Inspector was seated in deep cogitation.

Murder — by hand or hands unknown . . .

He himself was pretty sure that he knew the motive of the crime, though as yet he could prove nothing. He was not sure yet how many minds were behind the hand, but he believed more than one was.

The crime, he was convinced, was not over, but was still going on almost under his nose.

There were many factors still to be accounted for.

He suspected there might be a psychological puzzle of a baffling type . . .

And always in his sensitive and trained nose there was a peculiar smell — scent, aroma, perfume, if you liked — a sweet, cloying, sentimental odour seeming to associate itself with everything which had ever belonged to the deceased woman; reeking in her cupboards, among her clothes and papers; unmistakable, unidentifiable — emanating from no source he had as yet been able to trace . . .

He had thought he detected it on the torn strip of veil found in the garden; and when the whole of the veil was submitted to him, as he had requested, he was sure that he did . . .

Yet the veil was Mother Trevor's, and had nothing to do with Madame Sliema . . .

Or had it?

There was not a trace of this cloying scent anywhere but in the Guest House; but the Guest House was heavy with it. Mrs. Moss was heavy with it; Venetia gave it off. Now and then, to add to the puzzle, Sister Carmela's draperies seemed to waft it faintly . . .

It was not at all an unpleasant smell; rather the contrary . . . but cloying, and highly reminiscent of something . . .

The Inspector was sure he knew it well, but he could put no name on it.

And he dared not make inquiries, for it was of the essence of things at present that none but himself should be in the undivulged secret of its possibly evidential value.

16

ENTER A MALTESE BARON

By the terms of the only Will which anything but hypothesis knew anything about, the late Baroness Sliema had become a benefactress of the Convent, and, as such and in accordance with her testamentary wishes, she was given burial in the Convent cemetery.

The day of the funeral was that following the inquest, and a solemn Requiem Mass was sung by Mgr. Todhunter in the presence of the Community and school.

Present also — with, so to speak, a 'watching brief' — was the Inspector, occupying a prie-dieu in the side-chapel of the Immaculate Conception opposite the fatal one of St. Joseph.

It was not the Inspector, but Mr. Havelock Ellis, who said that even if the rite of Holy Mass were without validity, it would still be preserved wherever men love beauty as a supreme expression of human reverence and worship.

Certainly it was not at all in accordance with the Inspector's experience of a funeral ceremony. He had attended as many as most men of his age, and they usually left him void in mind and numb in body and full of a restless melancholy. This was his first Catholic funeral, however, and he was certainly impressed by the prominent position given to the coffin and the many beautiful attentions paid it. Again and again it was sprinkled with Holy Water and offered incense; again and again it was bowed to, blessed and visited. It seemed to the Inspector that Catholics are less afraid of their dead, less brusque with mortal remains, than are others; and the difference was pleasing to him.

The solemn Requiem proceeded; and the Inspector, from his point of vantage overlooking the altar from the side, watched, fascinated, the innumerable, elaborate and yet so swift actions of the priest's hands. The chapel was dim with incense and faint with the odours of the massed flowers. He wondered how in the world they contrived to teach such young boys as the acolyte seraphs to be so neat and prompt and circumspect in all their goings and comings. He greatly admired, too, the unaffected gravity of these youngsters, who, though they could know less than nothing about death, seemed yet with their wistful, pointed, almost expressionless little faces to have fathomed the very depths of human grief. There was something Chinese, he thought, about the solemn beauty of these robed boy-children as they worked the lovely pattern of the Mass.

Though his eyes did not wander from the altar or miss any action which was performed there, his mind took up the problem of old Madame Sliema's death. There it lay, what was left of that troublous, unlikable spirit, before him in its coffin, under all those flowers, the focus of all this funeral pomp; and there it might lie — not here, but in the grave — and no real harm be done if none ever knew who killed her. But the Law was inexorable in its demand for discovery and vengeance; society must be protected; and he, the Inspector, was the servant of society and the Law.

Besides, the Convent must not be left under the shadow of unsolved crime.

Where was that Will, that new Will, which he believed to be at the heart of the whole matter? Had it existed only in the mind of the dead woman? Or had it taken documentary form? If the latter, what had become of it? What did one do with a document to destroy which one had committed murder? Surely one put it into the nearest fire! There were no open fires at the Convent, and at this time of the year the furnaces were not alight; but there was a fire always in the kitchen, and usually in the laundries — and anyone could slip down there while the Sisters were at Mass. If all evidence of this motive had disappeared in flame, then the case had indeed an intractable look.

The priest had lifted up his hands.

'*Orate, fratres* . . . '

And a seraph answered him in a treble whisper:

'*Suscipiat Dominus sacrificium de manibus tuis . . .* '

An even deeper hush fell upon the congregation.

But why, the Inspector asked himself, had the so-called ghost walked? Why was Mother Trevor's habit stolen from the enclosure and returned smelling mysteriously of the apartments of the dead woman? That clue of his sensitive nose proved conclusively to the Inspector that either Mrs. Moss or Venetia had crept out on the night of the crime on some strange errand. Which? Venetia seemed by far the more likely. Yet her alibi for the crime seemed almost unassailable, and the Inspector was convinced that the murderer and the 'ghost' were one and the same person.

Or was it a conspiracy, involving more than one?

But who would conspire with old Mrs. Moss, half crazy in her head, subject to heart-attacks, and wholly crazy on her legs?

A chime of little bells sounded.

The seraphs had gravely risen and

surrounded the bending figure of the priest, raising the hem of his vestment.

The supreme moment of the Mass was approaching, and the Inspector bowed his head.

The bells chimed again. The priest knelt.

Again the bells chimed, and the priest rose, raising far above his head the Sacred Host.

The bells chimed again, and the Host was withdrawn.

Still the priest bent over the altar, again intimately muttering.

The bells chimed another profound genuflection — chimed the Sacred Cup high into the air — and for its return to the altar chimed a final chime.

Expressionless as ever, the seraphs silently arose and resumed their appointed stations on the altar steps.

In the silence which followed, the pouring of heavy rain could be heard outside, and the growl of thunder. Except where the candles shone upon the altar, it was very dark in the chapel. The beautiful May weather had broken in a storm.

Possibly the electricity in the atmosphere, the unfamiliar solemn beauty of what he had just seen and the tension of his own thoughts, had set the Inspector's nerves on edge, for he started and frowned when the door behind him was clumsily opened, and a young man in a blue raincoat stumbled in.

17

A MARRIAGE HAS BEEN ARRANGED

Any unexpected event following upon a long sequence of anxious thought is apt to seem like the fulfilment of prophecy. A glance round at the newcomer was enough to convince the Inspector that here was no other than the young Baron Sliema. It was not a very difficult deduction, for everything about the young man proclaimed the Mediterranean sea-board.

A police description of him would probably have run: *About or rather below the medium height, of slender build, sallow complexion, sleek black hair parted in centre, large nose and wispy moustache; wearing a dark blue double-breasted suit, etc. etc.*

The Inspector described him to himself as 'rather a seedy-looking specimen'. But this may have been merely stalwart British prejudice. Certainly the young man was of no athletic build; he looked, in fact, a little feeble and done-up, and his dark eyes had the petulant expression of nervous overstrain.

He very carefully pulled up his well-creased trousers before going uncomfortably down on one knee; and there he remained until the Mass was over, when he at once got up and went into the sacristy, engaging the attention of Mother Vannes.

If doubt there could have been, Mother Vannes's expression on seeing him would have dissolved it: this was the Baron Crauford Sliema.

The storm had passed over, though there was more of it hanging about — and now everything was being got ready for the procession to the graveside. A number of farm-men with 'Mock' Turtle at their head moved the coffin on to a wheeled trestle, and a moment later the young man was ushered in and took up his position as chief mourner.

The Inspector followed the procession,

at a little distance, down the avenue of trees from which great storm-drops were still falling after the recent downpour . . .

Mr. Turtle had not dug the grave, flatly declining to have anything to do with the proceedings; and, when told by Reverend Mother that he really was an 'impossible man', had argued at maddening length that it weren't possible to be impossible, and further that an impossible man couldn't dig no grave, so he couldn't. Reverend Mother, worsted as ever in any argument with Mr. Turtle, had repressed the wish that he would dig just one more grave and *get into it*!

Quarter of an hour later the remains of the old Baroness Sliema were in the grave, and the heavy earth was being thrown back on top of them. All her life through a giver of trouble, she had contrived to give a maximum in her death. Nothing could be more typical of her than that in the end she should get murdered for no reason anyone could see, and thereby upset all the functions of a large and busy establishment. If Reverend Mother returned to the house with a step buoyant rather than otherwise, who can blame her? The trying old lady was gone where she could be managed for her good.

With Reverend Mother walked the young Baron, to whom she was saying:

'How fortunate you were able to be here! Your presence is such a joy to poor old Mrs. Moss.'

The Baron considered this.

'Yes,' he agreed at length, 'no doubt I afford much satisfaction to my good foster-mother. This is natural — yes? It is natural that a nurse should love her babe . . . '

Reverend Mother privately thought it depended on the babe.

The young man was stroking his wispy moustache; it was plain that the subject of his foster-mother did not interest him, once he had got the fact syllogistically established that her emotions were a credit to her.

'This crime,' he said, 'it is very curious — yes? True, my mother was a disagreeable woman, but in a Convent one does not kill even these.'

(Meaning, thought Reverend Mother to herself, that there soon wouldn't be many of us left if one did!)

Aloud she said:

'You will have an opportunity of talking it over with the Inspector in charge.'

'Certainly,' agreed the Baron; 'with the police I must certainly have some conference.'

He added, with less of the perfect self-containment of a fish:

'But there is one, Madame, with whom I desire to confer much rather than with the police.'

'Mrs. Moss, no doubt?' suggested Reverend Mother.

She received a fish-like glance, and he answered in a petulant tone:

'For Mrs. Moss I entertain the natural sentiments of a babe for his nurse. But there is a young lady here, Madame — Miss Venetia Gozo . . . '

'Venetia!' exclaimed Reverend Mother. 'Is she a friend of yours?'

The Baron bowed gravely.

'If it shall not displease you, Madame, she is more than a friend. She is my heart

154

and my life. That young lady and myself, we entertain proposals of marriage between us. We are to be man and wife.'

'Bless me!' said Reverend Mother. 'I had no idea . . . '

'How should you have, Madame? It is in our mutual bosoms only that the truth is known. My mother, she is resolved against it; always she seclude my Venetia in a house of religion, where I cannot come. So unhappy are we that almost we decide to take together the iodine.'

'Iodine?' echoed Reverend Mother. 'But isn't that poison?'

'In Malta, Madame, when people are unhappy like this, it is the custom to take the iodine.'

'Good gracious!' said Reverend Mother.

The Baron twirled his inadequate moustache.

'*On ne badine pas*, Madame, *avec l'amour*. It is natural — yes? that two who entertain mutual sentiments of passion should wish to marry. But my mother, she is like a great rock in the pathway of our happiness . . . '

'Yes?' said Reverend Mother.

It was all she felt equal to at the moment. But all this certainly shed light on much that had been puzzling her about the girl Venetia. So the poor child had been in love the whole time — and with the wholly dependent son of her guardian! The situation must have given great scope to the old lady.

The Baron proceeded, a quite animated look in his eye.

'Me,' he said, 'she dismisses with a pittance to engage myself in the warfare of the General Franco. If I return without her leave, I forfeit this pittance, and she will disinherit me. None the less, Madame, such is my passion that I do return ... That is natural — yes? I address my mother by letter, imploring to see her. But she reply me with a shilling, and the flea in my ear that she summons her notaries to her side ... '

'You mean,' Reverend Mother said, 'that she told you she was going to make a new Will?'

The Baron bowed.

'I struggle, Madame, to be explicit

— plain, yes? Such is her intimation to me. I writhe in my anguish, but I am impotent: what can I do? Ah, Madame, but my Guardian Angel also is on the alert; in the act of disinheriting me my mother is struck down . . . '

'H'm,' said Reverend Mother.

She could not altogether accept this version of the facts.

By this time they had left the garden and were seated together in Reverend Mother's parlour.

'I explain to my mother,' proceeded the Baron, 'that I become tired of the warfare of Franco, and I wish to go to Rome to pursue there the studies of my father. For this I am well qualified.'

It was Reverend Mother's turn to bow. 'No doubt.'

She was thinking to herself, what a devastatingly smug young man! She was unacquainted with the Maltese male.

'I am well qualified,' pursued the Baron, 'except that I have no money. My mother, instead of desiring that I illustrate the name of Sliema with my genius and multiply it by the numerous offspring of myself and my Venetia, responds me only with the shilling and the threat of her notaries. Is this the part of a mother, Madame, towards her only child? I ask you . . . '

Reverend Mother had to admit that it was not.

'No, it was wrong of her: very unfair to you and Venetia. I only wish I had known about all this.'

'Pardon, Madame, but your knowledge it could have made no difference. Never will my mother have been persuaded to the happiness of myself and my Venetia. For me it is the warfare of Franco; for my Venetia it is the prison of your cloister. She is in the act of securing our everlasting separation by her revised testamentary dispositions when my Guardian Angel strikes her down.'

'H'm,' said Reverend Mother.

She was wondering how this theory of the crime would appeal to the Inspector.

The thought of the Inspector recalled Reverend Mother to several things: the need of seeing him — the charity of

158

sending Venetia at once to her lover . . .

She rose.

'You will excuse me. You can be quite at home here. I will send Venetia to you . . . '

The Baron had also risen, his sallow face illuminated. Sinking on one knee, he pressed his lips to Reverend Mother's hand, and characteristically burst into loud sobs.

'Ah, Madame, if you could know what those words mean to me . . . 'I will send to you your Venetia' . . . '

18

THE CHIEF-INSPECTOR
INTERRUPTS LOVE-PASSAGES

It is but seldom that the parlour of a Reverend Mother of a Convent is made into the scene of the reunion of lovers, but, as Reverend Mother herself remarked to the Inspector, *anything* was now possible at Harrington.

She described the Baron Crauford Sliema as well as she could (for she found him rather indescribable), and detailed all he had told her about his mother's expressed intentions.

'But I must say,' she concluded, 'if you are relying on Master Crauford for anything criminal, I am afraid you will be disappointed. I somehow don't see him in that light — or should it be darkness?'

'We shall see,' said the Inspector.

Being a bachelor, the Inspector knew nothing about how long an engaged couple should be left to themselves after a separation, and erred by presenting himself far too soon.

Venetia had only just time to settle her hair which had become disarranged by contact with the Baron's waistcoat buttons.

Though a bachelor, the Inspector was romantic, and he shared the general partiality for a lover and his lass. He came in smiling, apologising and offering congratulations. He much regretted at the moment that he strongly suspected the lady in the case of being the wanted lady in his own case.

The motive was now plain enough; the girl had acted in defence of her lover.

Her alibi notwithstanding — which, after all, rested on a general impression only — he was beginning to think that this sullen, black-browed girl might well prove to be the prime mover in the whole affair. He had been long enough at Harrington now to know that girls got about with extraordinary stealth and quickness . . .

It was a little awkward, he felt, to be offering congratulations to a young woman he was privately measuring for a noose.

He was greeted by the Baron with perfect equanimity and some condescension, but by the girl with looks of repulsion. Covertly he took note of her. She was short and full-busted; her hips and thighs were comely but thick; her hair was fuzzy, her complexion a waxy-white; her eyes, though admittedly large and houriesque, revealed no depth. She was the houri type externally, and as there was nothing of the Pasha in the Inspector she put him off.

Curiously enough, in the frail and brittle figure of the Baron there was any amount of the Pasha.

'I am Inspector Pearson,' said the Inspector. 'I am inquiring into the death of the late Baroness, your mother.'

'Yes,' replied Crauford, contriving somehow to make that familiar word sound very exotic; 'and what do you find, Inspector?'

The Inspector only smiled.

'You do not find very much, hein?' Crauford suggested in a cheerful voice. 'You are much in the dark — yes?'

His manner was almost jaunty, and it aggravated the Inspector.

'I am hoping, Baron, that you may be able to throw some light.'

Crauford shrugged his flexible shoulders.

'Me? What light can I throw? I know nothing.'

'You know, at any rate, that your mother was intending to alter her Will . . . '

'Intending! Ah yes. But she did not do so.'

The Inspector spoke with dryness.

'I am not so sure. I think it possible she may have done so.'

A greenish tinge appeared on Crauford's face; he got up and began pacing the room with nervous strides.

'But — but then — where is this Will? . . . '

'That is what I want to know. It may have been destroyed.'

Crauford relaxed slightly.

'Then all is again well,' he said.

The Inspector gave him a reproving glance.

'You don't seem to understand, Baron. This is a criminal investigation. Supposing such a Will to have existed — if I could find out who destroyed it, I think I could lay my hands on your mother's murderer.'

He stole, as he spoke, a glance at Venetia; but beyond profound concern for Crauford and dislike of himself, he could see no special consciousness.

Crauford was once more in jerky motion.

'But this is terrible — terrible! Venetia, you have no knowledge of this? . . . '

'I have none,' the girl replied. 'I do not believe it.'

The Inspector interposed.

'You lived in close touch with your late guardian, Miss Gozo. Considering also your engagement — I think you must have known something? . . . '

'I knew nothing.'

'Don't you mean, Miss Gozo — you will tell me nothing?'

'I mean what I say.'

The girl went on in a low, thick voice.

'It was the vanity of that one to be secret and sudden. To have us all at her mercy, under her hand — me — her son — Mrs. Moss . . . To arbitrate our destinies . . . It was the vanity of that one . . . '

Crauford, under this strain, was rapidly becoming hysterical.

'It is again the iodine for you and me, Venetia. She will rule us still from the grave.'

The girl took his limp hand, and cherished it.

'It is not so,' she said in her low, penetrating voice. 'Listen to the sound of the rain! . . . '

Outside the stormy downpour was renewed, and a wind thrashed among the trees.

The girl went on, thrillingly.

'Listen, Crauford, listen! The soil is sogging, sogging down on to her coffin, heavy and saturated with water. No, Crauford, no; she will not rise to spoil our happiness.'

She paused, and added through clenched teeth:

'She is dead.'

Involuntarily the Inspector shuddered; the way the words were spoken suggested not death but annihilation.

Crauford was on his knees, his head in Venetia's lap; he was, of course, sobbing bitterly.

'Yes, yes — she is dead. But you and I, Venetia, we are alive . . . '

'We are alive, Crauford — and young . . . '

The Inspector tactfully withdrew.

He was of Reverend Mother's opinion about Crauford; but the girl . . .

Everything pointed straight at her.

She had the mind, the motive, and he felt sure she had found the means.

19

VERITY MAKES HER BED WITH A VIEW TO LYING ON IT

Although it was only a few days since all the trouble started, already the Convent had quite settled down to its police occupation. Indeed it would be difficult to say whether the Convent were in charge of the police or the police in charge of the Convent. It is a tribute to the immense vitality of Harrington that its digestion proved fully equal to so foreign a body as the police.

For a day or two Mother Peck resented the large constables quartered in her lodge, but when she found that they ate out of her hand she became first reconciled to their presence and then positively fond of them.

The Priests' Parlour soon became known as the Inspector's Parlour.

The Inspector himself became inextricably mixed up in the minds of the younger children with His Grace the Archbishop. They were surprised that he gave them no homilies and did not appear at the altar in pontificals.

But, as Reverend Mother said, 'all this police business was ruinous to discipline'. Lessons were felt as an extra nuisance when you might be outside improvising some new version of Sleuths v. Nuns. Inez Escapado and Grazia Bombado were more than ever inclined to get above themselves. In the various class-rooms and common rooms the study of Latin Grammar and quadratic equations was increasingly neglected. Even School Certificate took a back place. The great and emergent question was, who killed old Madame Sliema? Even Thistle McBinkie and her coevals made less progress with the multiplication table.

As Torquilla put it to her fellow Ribbon Alauda:

'It's too thrilling to be actually living inside a thriller. What a sell for the Nuns!'

This graceless remark referred to the

fact that the reading of sensational literature is not encouraged at Convent schools.

Verity Goodchild was thirsting to distinguish herself, though it might well be thought that this young lady had already done enough. Mother Peagle was strongly of this opinion, and urged Verity to rest content with the laurels she had gained. It had been a great surprise to Mother Peagle when Verity was not turned out of her bedroom, and it was a greater when, going there on one occasion, she found the tenant busily engaged, with the help of Torquilla, Prudence, Alauda, Jamette and Philomene, in changing the position of the bed.

But before she could get out a word she was overwhelmed in full chorus:

'It's all right, Mother; we were just coming to tell you. The Inspector said so, and Reverend Mother O.K.'d it.'

Mother Peagle had never expected to see such a day; it was enough to deceive, if possible, even the elect. But all she said, as she set about to help, was:

'You know I dislike Americanisms. Why cannot you say Reverend Mother *confirmed* it?'

'But only a Bishop can confirm, Mother,' Verity remarked with apparent innocence.

But Mother Peagle was not taken in, and it was some relief to her feelings to give the young lady an imposition consisting of fifty well-written lines to the following effect:

I must strive prayerfully not to be pert.

'Oh, *Mother!*' expostulated the injured one.

But Mother Peagle had sailed out of the room, leaving the others to administer Job's comfort to Verity.

Torquilla, with her strong arms, put a finishing touch to the re-made bed in its new position.

'How's that, Verity?'

Verity broke the strict rule of the school against lying on a bed during the day.

'Super,' was her comment.

All the others experimented in turn, and agreed. By only turning her head on the pillow Verity could now command a full view of the Ghost's Walk.

'Oo,' shuddered Philomene, 'whatever *would* you do, Verity?'

Verity owed the Ribbons one for their undissimulated pleasure in her imposition. She answered Philomene with biting sarcasm:

'Call a Ribbon at once. Do you suppose a little girl like me could do anything?'

Jamette and Philomene were delighted at this thrust, while the Ribbons looked haughtily down the sides of the nose.

'Yes, and I bet you jolly well would,' Torquilla said. 'The obvious person would be myself, as I'm hockey captain.'

'Why? Do you suppose the ghost plays hockey?'

'Don't be a worse ass than you can help. As hockey captain, I am accustomed to taking charge. Besides, I've got biceps . . . '

She rolled up her sleeve, displaying considerable firm plumpness.

'If you don't believe it's biceps,' she added, 'just have a look at Philomene's.'

'Than't,' said Philomene, backing out

of harm's way, beset by lisps.

'Oh bother your biceps,' put in Alauda. 'Tell us what you really *would* do, Verity.'

Verity looked as demure as her particular type and tilt of nose permits.

'Depend upon it, dear child,' she answered Alauda, 'I have my instructions. None of you little Ribbons will know anything about it until next morning. The Inspector and Reverend Mother — in consultation with myself — are particularly anxious to avoid panic among the Ribbons and the bab — '

But at this point she was upset over the bed, a pillow placed on her head, and sat on.

'Dear me, dear me!' said the voice of Mother Peagle at the door. 'What is all this? Three Ribbons present, and all this noise and romping . . . '

'It was Philomene, Mother,' gasped Verity, struggling up on the bed. 'She wouldn't let us feel her biceps . . . '

'We are very sorry, Mother,' said the Ribbons with downcast eyes.

'That is always the tale I am told. All of you must leave this room at once. Verity, I shall expect those lines before supper . . . '

'Oh Mother, have a heart . . . '

But Mother Peagle declined to have a heart; and Verity dwindled off downstairs with a suffering expression. Jamette and Philomene went with her as moral support.

On their way along the corridors Jamette resumed the importuning of Verity.

'Verity, do tell just Phil and me what you would do . . . '

'Oh pleath, Verity,' sighed Philomene.

Verity rejoined kindly.

'Do you really want to know? . . . '

'Oh you *darling*! . . . '

Arms were thrown around Verity's neck, and ears advanced to her lips.

'Take your ears away, children,' said Verity; 'so few of them are washed. Well, if the ghost appears . . . '

'If the ghost appears!' they echoed.

'In that case — ' Verity was beginning; but she got no further.

A tall, black shadow loomed over them, and a grim voice said:

'Are you aware that you are *not* to talk in the corridors?'

It was Mother Bassonthwaite, perhaps the most to be dreaded of all the Mothers in the school.

'Yes, Mother . . . '

'Then how have you the audacity to do it! Were you children going anywhere?'

'To the Senior Library, Mother . . . '

'Proceed then, in orderly fashion and the strictest silence; and, on arrival, write out for me in your least abominable handwriting that beautiful poem of Wordsworth's, beginning:

'*Stern Daughter of the Voice of God . . . *''

Jamette and Philomene were paralysed by this blow, but Verity managed to moan out:

'Oh, Mother, I've got one imposition already . . . '

Mother Bassonthwaite glimmered down from her intimidating height with the thin, pale smile of utter ruthlessness.

'I am not surprised to hear it. Now you have two. Be careful not to incur a third.'

With which Mother Bassonthwaite resumed her awful prowl along the corridor.

20

MRS. MOSS

There was still storm in the air, but for the moment the sun shone again. Old Mrs. Moss, under the gentle compulsion of Mother Trevor, was helped out into the garden, where she was seated on a carefully dried garden-seat with a parasol in order to enjoy a breath of such air as there was.

It was obvious that she was little pleased to be joined there by the Inspector.

He was, on his side, as little pleased to have to plague the poor old soul, but duty is duty. Fortunately, the gentle way he had with him and his perfect patience reassured Mrs. Moss by degrees.

The Inspector was a long time in coming anywhere near the point. At last he said:

'It must be a great joy to you, Mrs.

Moss, to have the Baron here . . . '

'It is a joy, sir — yes. Poor Crauford! I nursed him, sir, as a baby. He was an ailing child . . . '

'He seems well now,' the Inspector hazarded.

The old lady answered with what the Inspector thought remarkable intelligence.

'I hope he may be, sir — now. He will have at least half of his patrimony — and now they tell me he is engaged to Venetia . . . '

'You did not know that?' suggested the Inspector.

She sighed, and shook her head.

'I knew — so little, about Crauford. Though Madame did not love him, she was angry that I should . . . '

'Miss Gozo did not confide in you?'

'Confide? Oh my dear sir, she knew better than that. I am old and weak and ill . . . There was nothing Madame could not have got out of me. No, she did not confide. Poor girl, why should she?'

There was a note of such hapless, passive suffering in the way she spoke that the Inspector's innate delicacy was much daunted. He almost felt he did not want to know the story which lay behind those words and the voice in which they were spoken. But Inspectors are not allowed to indulge delicate feelings.

He resumed quietly.

'You were not in Miss Gozo's confidence? That does not surprise me. She seems a very self-sufficient young woman.'

To his surprise, and almost consternation, the old woman made a throaty sound which was a laugh.

'Self-sufficient? She had need be. All women had need be, but they seldom are. Self-sufficient . . . '

She was thinking, the Inspector perceived, of her own long, servile and dependent life.

She went on:

'Yes, Venetia is no weakling. She would not have gone under — as I did. But Crauford is weak — weak as water . . . '

She broke off, and added:

'Why do I talk of this? It is not what

you want of me. What is it you want of me? . . . '

This clear insight into his designs disconcerted the Inspector, and he resumed awkwardly.

'I want all you can tell me — more than you have as yet told me. I am convinced you have not told me all you know . . . '

The old woman sighed, and shifted her sunshade.

'Why should I hide anything from you? Very soon I shall be dead. Yes, yes, the doctor says so. So near the judgment of God, why should I hide anything? . . . '

'Because,' the Inspector said, 'of Crauford . . . '

Again she made that throaty noise which was a kind of ghastly laugh.

'I am so foolish — yes? I am a silly, crazy old woman? I can see that Crauford cares — nothing — for me? . . . '

'Surely you misjudge him,' said the Inspector.

'I do not judge him, and so I cannot misjudge him.'

The Inspector spoke more quietly than ever.

'But you *love* him? . . . '

'And if I do? It is another of life's tricks . . . '

'If you do,' almost whispered the Inspector, 'you would help him — yes, even if he is ungrateful.'

His voice sank lower still.

'Mrs. Moss, tell me, for I am sure you know — what was in that Will which you destroyed? . . . '

She terrified him by almost leaping, all tremulous as she was, to her feet.

'*Before God, I destroyed no Will . . .* '

She subsided, her face working, her lips an ominous cyanose.

'Tell me, then,' said the Inspector, his fingers involuntarily finding her feeble pulse, 'where is that Will which she made? Tell me . . . '

She muttered.

'It is — with her — in the grave. Is she not dead, and are not her purposes dead with her?'

'You admit, she had — purposes? . . . '

'Always she had purposes. But her purposes are in the grave. I tell you, she is dead. Someone struck her down . . . '

'Mrs. Moss, do you know who struck her down? . . . '

'God struck her down . . . '

'Mrs. Moss, try to calm yourself. Let us speak of this sensibly. God acts through agents . . . '

The old woman cried out:

'She is dead, and you would raise her! Oh God, if you had known her! Man, man, I have told you all . . . God struck her, and her evil will is in the grave . . . '

The figure of Mother Trevor was seen coming back up the avenue after her daily walk in the grounds.

'Dear Mrs. Moss, you have been exciting yourself — talking to the Inspector. Perhaps he will give you his arm, and I will give you mine; it is time you went to lie down.'

The Inspector, with a sense of abject guilt, was all compassionate alacrity. They got the trembling old woman to the Guest House door, and with even greater care up the stairs leading to her room.

Mother Trevor went in with the patient. The Inspector went down to the Priests'

Parlour, where Sister Carmela was busy getting his tea.

It all seemed quite plain to him.

There *had* been a Will disinheriting Crauford. Mrs. Moss had known of it, and so had Venetia. There was far, far more underlying all this than he as yet understood, but one thing seemed certain —

Venetia had acted.

21

VERITY BAFFLES CURIOSITY

It was still the day of the funeral — towards evening now, after a tigerish day of tawny sunshine and black storm.

The Inspector was fond of seeing analogies in the weather and in the behaviour of the natural creation, and it struck him as he looked out that evening that the sudden calm which had fallen was almost too complete, like the quiet fit of a maniac. The birds did not trust it, for they raised no song.

Mr. Turtle did not trust it either, and remarked as much to Mrs. Turtle and Mock when he turned in for a substantial high tea.

' 'Tisn't what I would call *likely* weather,' he said, as he pulled up his chair to table and stuck a voluminous napkin in his shirt-collar. 'Rain is good, and sun is good, coming regular and alternate, like;

but extremes is to be avoided in the 'igher atmospheres as elsewhere. Blazes is bad, and soaks is bad . . . '

'Ah,' rejoined Mrs. Turtle, as she dished up, 'trouble with you, Turtle, is, and ever have been, as you would like to be the Lord.'

Mr. Turtle did not reply; the thing was just the sort of unsubtle repartee to be expected of a woman. There were many aspects of the Lord's work, such as the stars in their courses, which Mr. Turtle abstained from criticising, but he did feel that, strictly in the gardening line, he might now and then have offered a useful hint.

In the graveyard the new mound of earth had been almost flattened out by the rain. The flowers of the many wreaths had been beaten to pieces, so that the ugly wire framework showed.

It had been a little difficult to suggest to Crauford Sliema that Reverend Mother might like to have back the use of her parlour, but by degrees the thing was done, and now the Baron had gone back to his hotel in Bloomsbury

— where, on arrival, much to the disgust of Mother Peck, he had promptly rung up Venetia.

Mother Peck had also been considerably scandalised by the unabashed embraces of the lovers on parting in the lodge.

Venetia was a changed girl. She no longer moved about soundlessly like a nun but walked briskly with an assertive tap of the heels. She no longer muted her voice in speaking, but spoke up and out. She received Reverend Mother's congratulations, and those of other nuns, with an air of hauteur. It was clear that Crauford not only filled her heart but had gone slightly to her head.

The Inspector kept an unobtrusive eye on her whereabouts. He was very sorry for her.

At him, when she happened to see him, Venetia directed a glance of open scorn. He admired her for it.

And still, and in spite of repeated onslaughts, that 'brave Horatius' of a Verity Goodchild 'kept the bridge' of her sealed orders against 'all the ranks of

Tusculum'. Though Torquilla declared she would never stop trying, and Philomene moaned that she was probably dying, and everybody said something, and most people the same thing more than once, and even bribes were attempted, still all they got out of Verity was that particularly bright smile so often seen on the faces of people who definitely hold the upper hand.

At supper a semi-final, and at bedtime a final effort was made by all. They gathered wistfully just outside Verity's door, offering gifts and personal services of all kinds, and keeping a sharp look-out for one of Mother Peagle's famous bat-swoops or ectoplasmic materialisations out of the void.

'Oh, Verity, you *might* . . . '

'Oh, Verity, oh *do* . . . '

'Be a sport, Verity . . . '

And from Philomene:

'It'th cruelty, Verity. I than't thleep a wink if you don't . . . '

Verity stood in the doorway, beaming affectionately at the plaintive faces, pirouetting on the extreme tips of her toes, and answered in the exact tones of Mother Peagle:

'My dear children, all this shows a bad spirit . . . in Ribbons a most unworthy spirit. I am quite sure you mean no disrespect, but that is what it amounts to. Of course I realize it is trying for you, but life, children, is full of trials. They are sent us for our good. You do not understand this yet, but you will. Be thankful, at present, that the burden of your lives is borne by those who have your welfare deeply at heart . . . '

At this point Torquilla stuffed a ball of wool she was carrying into Verity's mouth, and there was a chorus of profoundly personal insults.

One by one they lagged off to their respective rooms, and got into bed, resigning themselves to the pangs of unsated curiosity.

Philomene was resolved not to close an eye all night, so that her wan complexion and haggard eyes might reproach Verity next morning. But Nature overruled her. She had to be content with excluding Verity's name from her petitionary prayers that night.

None the less the whole thing had been a great strain on Verity, whose natural bias was all towards 'telling it out among the heathen' — with those added touches which made it so much more thrilling for the heathen. She was not at all sure how long she could keep this discretion business up.

On her knees at the bedside she adverted to the subject on high, and, after invoking the aid of her Patron Saint and Guardian Angel in all matters tending to salvation, she added:

'And, if at all possible — if there's going to be any fun . . . I mean, if I am to be called to any special service, in thy mercy let it happen before — '

She ransacked her mind for some more becoming expression, but reflected that her Guardian Angel would probably understand, whatever her Patron Saint might do.

' — Before,' she added, 'I spill the beans.'

22

THE GHOST AGAIN!

During term Mother Peagle did not enjoy the privacy and peace of the conventual enclosure. Her place was in the thick of things, ready at a moment's notice to waylay a sleep-walker and cope with the thousand and one corporal ills which beset children's insides during the night watches.

She slept therefore very lightly.

It might have been slightly past midnight that same night when Mother Peagle was — not startled, for nothing startled her, but certainly roused, to find a slight figure in pyjamas standing by her bed.

Its eyes were enormous, its mouth was half open, its arms and legs seemed strung on wires.

'My child! What is it? . . . '

Teeth chattered in reply.

'It — it's me, Mother. Verity. And, oh Mother, I've *seen* it *again! The ghost . . . it's gone down the path! Oh Mother . . .* '

Mother Peagle returned silent thanks that her own teeth were a denture, and not at present in, or otherwise they might have chattered like Verity's.

Her hands twitched, however, and her face was ashen, as she replied:

'There is nothing to be afraid of, my child. Put your trust absolutely in God. I shall be ready in a moment.'

The habit is not a thing which can be just thrown on, and the night-attire of a nun is hardly less dignified than the habit. Nevertheless Mother Peagle dressed herself fully, following an instinct which every policeman would understand. It is said that policemen could never do their multiform difficult and dangerous jobs without the moral support of the helmet.

Perfectly calm and collected again, Mother Peagle consoled the whimpering Verity.

'Wrap yourself up in the blankets, child; and wait here till I come back . . . '

'Oh, Mother . . . '

For the first time in her life Verity was very loth to part with Mother Peagle.

Mother Peagle passed silently through the dark corridors on her way to report to Reverend Mother.

Reverend Mother, too, was a light sleeper. She was up in an instant, and had roused several of the senior nuns.

It happened — not at all by luck, but by good management — that the Inspector was on the premises that night, occupying the Priests' suite in the Guest House, — and so Reverend Mother was able to say:

'Let the Inspector know by the house telephone. Keep Verity with you.'

But before leading her force into action, Reverend Mother opened the door of Mother Trevor's room and looked in. Mother Trevor was fast asleep, and all things were disposed in rightness around her. But Reverend Mother glided into the room.

When she came back, she whispered to Mother Peagle and the others:

'*Her other habit is gone.*'

They nodded significantly.

Next minute Reverend Mother and her chosen few had set off in pursuit of the ghost.

Hardly more than three minutes had elapsed since Verity awoke Mother Peagle.

A minute more, and the Inspector was sitting up in bed listening to a clear but recessive voice which informed him by telephone of the turn events had taken.

He hopped quite youthfully out of bed.

'Splendid, Mother; splendid! Is all well in the house?'

All was well, replied the clear but recessive voice.

The Inspector dressed in haste, but he did not put on his boots. He thrust a powerful torch into a pocket.

He did not know what the game was, but he thought he was pretty sure who was playing it.

And that person was playing it once too often!

Avoiding the *Pons Asinorum* of a Conventually elbow-greased wooden flooring, he descended his private staircase, took a few steps along the corridor, and, his heart rather lumpish in his throat, began to mount the stairs leading to the Ladies' Guest Rooms, where had slept old Madame, and still slept Mrs. Moss and — Venetia Gozo . . .

'Why do the Gentiles rage and the people devise vain things?' . . .

Yes, and why do young women quit their warm beds in the chilly small hours to haunt a dripping garden in disguise?

In the lodge the two constables, always on duty there, were scratching their pates over a Crossword Puzzle, which announced that a prize of £5,000 positively must be won.

'Ah,' said one, 'and I wish it must be yours truly . . . '

'Ah,' said the other, who was a man of few words.

Verity all this while continued to sit on Mother Peagle's bed with hammering heart. How she longed for company — even at the price of having to say the Rosary, which would probably be Mother Peagle's idea!

It was so dark, and the queer oppression of so much slumber all around her daunted Verity. The whole house was haunted with phantasms of the night, and everybody in it was eerily forth from her waking self.

It was with tears of relief that Verity greeted Mother Peagle's return, and the tears were not rebuked. Nor was the Rosary mooted. Nor had Mother Peagle, in her silent and vigilant tour of the entire school, neglected to bring Verity something to eat and drink. Nor did Mother Peagle fail to speak affectionately, cheerfully, reassuringly.

'This can't be the old Peaglums,' Verity thought, as she found her weakness remembered and her needs sustained.

But it was in fact that very same 'Peaglums', whose fussiness for their welfare all the girls derided. It was the circumstances that were different: that was all.

A little time passed by; and again Mother Peagle glided off on a tour of inspection, leaving a much-restored Verity behind her.

Mother Peagle was never sure afterwards if she heard the garden-door of the

Guest House open. What she certainly did hear was groans of pain proceeding from the room of old Mrs. Moss. They were heart-rending, bespeaking a very bad attack.

Mother Peagle hurried there. Half-dressed, Mrs. Moss was lying collapsed on a dishevelled bed; her face and lips were the colour of death, and her eyes were dilated with fear . . .

Mother Peagle snatched up the brandy-flask and the bottle of prescribed drops . . .

For a while it looked like touch and go, but then the old woman seemed to become easier. Her head rolled over on the pillow, and her eyes closed.

Mother Peagle flew off to ring up the infirmary, but in the passage downstairs she was waylaid.

A sombre group of nuns was reassembling there, among them Reverend Mother.

A cock of Mother Peagle's head was enough, and Reverend Mother answered at once:

'No luck! . . . '

'Where is the Inspector?' someone asked.

But no one answered, for no one knew.

23

WHAT HAD BECOME OF THE INSPECTOR?

The Inspector was a man of the highest and most responsible moral character.

Never before in all his professional and private life had he lurked outside the bedroom door of a young and attractive girl. He had never felt the urge. He did not feel it now; quite the contrary. With all his heart he wished he could have deputed this particular bit of investigation. He would far rather have faced a desperate gang of 'toughs', revolvers in hand, than enter this chamber of chastity — empty as he knew it to be!

None the less he did it. Duty is duty.

Noiselessly he opened the door, and peered into the darkness of the room. It seemed to him very dark indeed — almost unnaturally dark; and it breathed forth that cloying scent with which his nose was already so familiar.

There was very little furniture. The bed was a mere white glimmer in the corner by the window.

The Inspector was a brave man — on occasion, even a dashing man; he had served all through the war and received well-deserved decorations. But one adventure he had shirked — or at least never attempted; he had never married. The celibacy of the clergy is one thing, but a detective ought to be married; he ought not to be quite so utterly daunted as the Inspector was by a feminine atmosphere.

Were those really — er — *stockings* hanging over the back of that chair! . . .

When a man is not used to it, crawling on all fours is an awkward feat. The Inspector had had very little of this kind of practice. It struck him, as he tried unsuccessfully to get something of the rhythm of a snake into his movements, that he was getting elderly. Perhaps it would soon be time to make way for a younger man with stronger abdominal muscles.

The prospect of early retirement did not cheer him; he heaved a heavy sigh.

There was a sharp click — an upheaval of bedclothes — a shrill exclamation . . .

The light was switched on, and an indignant young woman sat bolt upright among the sheets and pillows, regarding the Inspector as if he were the very snake he had striven so unsuccessfully to imitate!

It was a tableau — the girl upright and indignant, the Inspector crouching and ashamed!

No doubt it is a shock to a virtuous young girl to find a man crawling across her bedroom floor. If Venetia's eyes had had the same effect as Diana's on Actaeon, the chances are the Inspector would have trotted out on four feet. As it was, he stayed crouched.

It was of course the outraged damsel who spoke.

'*Mr. Inspector!* . . . '

The Inspector said nothing.

'I am aware that the police have rights . . . that they are entitled . . . that it may be their duty — but *really* . . . '

Her voice was scathing.

The Inspector made no reply; he had begun a backward movement on the model of his approach.

'I know you suspect me,' stormed Venetia. 'I would have answered any questions at a proper time. But to enter my bedroom at midnight . . . Is this the Third Degree? . . . '

The Inspector took the advice he had given to so many criminals, and said nothing.

Venetia threw herself back on the pillows in a passion of sobs.

'If I am to be arrested I ought at least to be warned. I am entitled to legal advice and the presence of my fiancé. Is this Nazi Germany? . . . '

With a cautious foot the Inspector was feeling for the door.

Venetia rallied and sat bolt upright again.

'Go,' she cried wildly, 'go! If you are a gentleman, and not just a policeman, go . . . '

The Inspector was in a position to oblige her; he had reached the door, and was backing through it.

He was almost through, and was closing the door quietly when Venetia, in a transport of modesty, burst out of bed, bounded across the room, and banged it behind him.

The Inspector said nothing.

A man of few words, on this occasion he had surpassed himself.

24

ORANGE FLOWER WATER

When Reverend Mother met Sister Carmela in the cloister next morning she saw at once that she must stop and say a word.

The whole of the Sister's body was keyed up to a high note of mute entreaty.

'Well, Sister Carmela, how goes it with your department this bright morning? How is the Inspector?'

Sister Carmela made her profound curtsey with a low chuckle and ravishing ogle of the great eyes, in love of Reverend Mother and satisfaction at gaining her desire. But immediately afterwards her face became a picture of dolour, almost despair; her hands were thrust a little in front of her as if deprecating fate, and she seemed to shrink to half her natural size.

'Oh, Reverend Mother, de Inspector is *not* well!'

She made a beautiful little sad melody of the words.

'He does not eat de good sausages for his breakfast!'

She contrived somehow to *act* the Inspector not eating the good sausages, so that the full pathos of it was brought home to Reverend Mother.

Sister Carmela continued on a note of rising tragedy.

'He does not read de newspaper. But always he sit with de head on de hand looking *oh* so sad!'

Her voice broke, and real and very large tears brimmed her eyes.

Reverend Mother was deeply moved.

'Cheer up, Sister dear. I am sure he will soon be all right again. Men do get things so badly on their minds, poor things, don't they?'

Sister Carmela ogled appreciation of this, and then swept a profound gesture of sorrow which seemed not for the Inspector only but for all suffering mankind.

'If *Reverend Mother* would speak to him,' she supplicated, 'den I am sure he will eat up de good sausages.'

'Well, well,' said Reverend Mother; and, leaving the Sister exultant, she went to the Priests' Parlour.

The Inspector did indeed look mopy. The sausages were untouched; even the tea in his cup was cold and filmy. The newspaper lay unfolded at his elbow, which was on the table among the knives and forks supporting a heavy head. He only wanted a few potsherds, Reverend Mother thought, to be the very picture of Job!

'Good morning, Mr. Inspector. Why, what is this?'

Her eyes surveyed the table.

He raised a haggard face towards her, which had none the less lit up with a forlorn gleam of hope.

'I — I hadn't the heart . . . '

Reverend Mother refrained from the retort that the heart is not the organ concerned with breakfast. All she said was — but she said it in a special way:

'What is the matter? Tell me . . . '

He passed his hand over his eyes several times.

'Only, that I have blundered. I am a failure. It is time I retired. I do not seem to — take hold — the way I once did . . . '

Reverend Mother saw that this was not a case to be dealt with in a hurry; she sat down. This was her first discouraged policeman, but she knew all about discouraged novices. With unerring instinct she came straight to the point.

'*You* getting an old man! *Your* powers failing! My dear Mr. Inspector, you must excuse me if I say what utter nonsense! Where the higher powers of the mind and soul are concerned, you are still a young man. Look at the Holy Father! Very few are elected under sixty.'

It was rather like pumping up a tyre, she thought.

'As for not taking hold . . . why, you have only been in this puzzling place a few days, and already you know us all by name and reputation. You know something of our Rule and way of life. You know the school almost as well as Mother Peagle herself. You are a lesson to us all. And you tell me you are a failure! I suppose you mean you have not yet solved this mystery? . . . '

'No,' said the Inspector, 'it isn't that. I *have* solved it, only — only — '

Reverend Mother did not exclaim, though she felt much excited.

'Why, then — ' was all she said.

'Only,' pursued the Inspector, 'I have blundered so unpardonably. The thing was plain enough to me from the start, but I would not believe. I feel sure my arteries are hardening . . . '

'Nothing of the sort,' said Reverend Mother firmly.

'When I say I have solved the mystery,' pursued the Inspector, 'I do not mean I have *proved* it. I could not ask for a Warrant . . . '

He broke off, still clutching at his hair — and added:

'But I *shall* prove it — and before the day is over!'

'Of course,' said Reverend Mother. 'That is the way I like to hear a man talk.'

She permitted herself to add:

'And so our mystery is solved. You know who killed old Madame Sliema? . . . '

The Inspector suddenly thumped the table with his fist, a gesture totally unlike him.

'God struck her down,' he said in a loud voice; 'and her evil will is in the grave with her . . . '

Reverend Mother dissimulated the real anxiety she felt for his mind. He was only saying what all the Community had thought all along, but, coming from him, it was different.

The Inspector calmed down quickly.

'Forgive my manners. I am not mad — really I am not. It is only — what a fool I have been! . . . '

'We all are sometimes,' Reverend Mother said. 'I only wish you could have seen *us* in the garden last night! It was funny beyond words. Set a nun to catch a nun! Such a Blindman's Buff you never saw! . . . and all of us perfectly in character! I really feel we owe it to the Junior School to repeat the performance some fine evening . . . '

She ran on lightly, giving the Inspector time to get over that feeling that his arteries were hardening.

'And now,' she concluded, 'don't you think you could manage just a little breakfast if I — '

But the Inspector firmly shook his head.

'No, really. I am better without. What I should really like — '

He broke off to say anxiously:

' — I am not a drinker as a rule, but — '

Reverend Mother suppressed a smile.

' — but what I should really like is a glass of wine and a few dry biscuits. Then I am going out to complete this case. I must speak to Mr. Turtle . . . '

Again Reverend Mother feared for his mind.

'I may have to commit a bit of sacrilege, but it can't be helped. If I could have a glass of wine and a few dry biscuits . . . ?'

His wishes were soon gratified.

But when he had poured out a glass of wine and was munching a dry biscuit, the irresistibly pleading voice of Sister Carmela made itself heard from the sideboard where she lingered.

In one hand she held a spotlessly clean bit of rag, and in the other a bottle without a label.

She proffered both to the Inspector.

'If de Signu',' she said, 'would but wet de rag from de bottle, and put on above de eyes . . . oh how refreshing that is! . . . '

She rolled her eyes heavenwards, with a beatific expression.

The Inspector was touched.

'Why, Sister,' he said, taking the bottle, 'what is it?'

Sister Carmela spoke proudly.

'It is de producement of my country — of Malta. Old Madame, she has lived in Malta and learn there to make it. Never she is without oh much of it, which we keep for her in de cellars . . . '

She closed her eyes and threw back her head, convincingly acting the effects of her prescription.

'Oh, lovely!' she exclaimed.

The Inspector uncorked the bottle, sniffed, and nearly fell off his chair.

If the bottle had contained pure

ammonia, he could not have sounded more breathless.

'*What — what is this? . . .* '

'Ah, you like it — yes? I think so. It is de producement of my lovely island home. It is de very best orange flower water of Malta . . . '

There was a pause, during which the Inspector washed forehead and stinging eyes with the ineffably soft and fragrant lotion, while Sister Carmela watched in a trance of affectionate and patriotic ecstasy.

Perhaps there is no sweetness in the world to be compared to the sweetness of the orange flower — where it stars the sturdy trees of Malta, in enclosed, sun-hoarding gardens, where flagged paths lead to old and curious fountains . . .

And this was the distilled essence of those starry flowers!

It does not cloy when fresh — any more than the nuptials of which it is the symbol.

It is a bridal sweetness, full of chimes and poignant memories . . .

It is clinging, like the arms and lips of youth enchanted . . .

Stale, it is fusty . . .

It was that smell which the Inspector had striven in vain to identify!

25

A MINOR MYSTERY CLEARED UP
– VERITY IS UNMASKED

Something was always happening in this hard world to make Philomene cry.

She had waked that morning in the full and happy hope of soon finding out Verity's secret, and found instead that Verity had mysteriously vanished into the infirmary!

Mother Peagle said that Verity had a bad headache and could not be visited just now.

It sent Philomene off into fountains of tears.

It was perfectly true that Verity had a headache, though in the ordinary way she would just have had to put up with it. As things were, Reverend Mother had jumped at the chance of temporarily segregating so unreliable a repository of official secrets. It would never do if the school got to know of the night's proceedings, for already there were whispers enough that the spirit of old Madame Sliema did not rest in the grave. If such a story got about in the junior dormitories, there would be no end to it — though there would almost certainly be a speedy end to poor Mother Peagle!

So Verity's headache was distinguished with a visit to the infirmary.

And Philomene wept pints of tears.

All during Mass they trickled down her pale little face. It was not the disappointment only, but she was sure Verity was very ill.

The truth was that Verity had made a fine breakfast of sausages, and was now snuggling off to sleep again, congratulating herself on skipping Morning Meditation, Mass, and very likely all lessons for the day.

Mother Infirmarian, for her own sake, tenderly encouraged her patient's drowsiness.

But Philomene looked so peaky, and rejected breakfast with such emphatic asperity, that Mother Peagle sent her out into the garden to try what a breath of fresh air would do. Philomene was fond of lone excursions, during which she habitually talked to herself.

'You poor thing! What a lot you have to put up with, you poor, poor thing! Never mind, dear; do cheer up . . . '

She used two quite different voices for the complaints and the comfort.

The Inspector, on his way to hunt up Mr. Turtle, was much upset to overhear so sad a dialogue proceeding from behind a bush. It was sad, and yet very touching, he thought, the way the one little girl consoled the other. He wondered what was the matter, and if he could do anything to set it right.

The voices continued:

'Life is such a swiz! Just when you think it's going to be nice, it turns out nasty. Yes, darling, but try to be a brave girl; perhaps things aren't quite so bad as you think . . . '

The Inspector was not proof against this; he did a bit of inspecting on the other side of the bush, and great was his astonishment to find only one little girl where he was quite sure there ought to be two.

The truth of the matter was not long in dawning upon him however, and it seemed more pathetic still. Poor little thing! . . .

'Why, my child,' he said, 'what is it?'

Philomene was unabashed, because her dialogues were entirely unconscious. She screwed up her negligible body into even smaller compass, and gave the Inspector such a look out of brimming, dove-blue eyes that he longed with all his heart to pick her up.

'It isn't anything,' she murmured; 'only I am *miserable* — *beyond* — *all words* . . . '

It sounded to the Inspector more like something!

'Is there anything,' he hesitated, 'I could do to help?'

The only idea in his head was those very sugary, bilious, squidgy buns which girls are usually so fond of, — but in this respect the Convent garden was no better than a desert.

But Philomene's petals were opening; it

had just dawned upon her that this nice, sympathetic person was the Head Sleuth. Supposing she could have a secret of her own — and refuse darkly to divulge it either to Verity or the Ribbons —

Meanwhile she continued to rend the Inspector's heart by looking small, fragile, sorrowful and — yes, there is only the one word for it where any man is concerned — *pretty!*

She confided in the Inspector.

'My best friend has gone into the infirmary with an awful bad illness. You know her? She is the girl who was to look out for the ghost . . . '

'My dear child,' said the Inspector, 'believe me, there are no such things as ghosts.'

'No, of course,' Philomene said; but she did not look convinced.

She began to lisp badly.

'Verity wath tho funny all yethterday. The wouldn't tell what the had to do if the thaw — no, not a ghotht, but — anything. It wath tho unlike Verity . . . and now the ith tho ill . . . '

The lower lip trembled again, the

dove-blue eyes brimmed; and the poor bamboozled Inspector himself was on the brink of tears.

He had however a vivid recollection of the interesting invalid in question — he had in fact carefully cut out the *Peephole* pictures — and somehow he felt a full confidence in her stamina and recovery.

'Perhaps she isn't so very bad,' he reassured Philomene. 'And if it's worrying you what she is to do if she ever — er — sees anything, I can tell you . . . '

'*Oh you angel!* . . . '

The Inspector had never before been called an angel, but he was not averse from new experiences.

Quietly he explained to Philomene.

'It did not amount to very much. There was no danger at all in it. If your friend happened from her window to see anything — ah — at all out of the ordinary, she had simply to report the matter to — I forget the name of your good mistress; to — er — to — ah — Mother Peagle . . . '

Philomene had shot to her feet, all the

crushed flower look gone out of her. The serpent not the dove was in her eye. There was not a trace of a lisp in the voice with which she answered.

'Of all the beastly rotten humbugs! And her pretending I don't know what — just to tantalize us! I'll never speak to that girl again as long as I live. I hope she just *is* ill, and it *hurts*. Thanks ever so much for telling me, but all is over between Verity and me *for ever*.'

The Inspector sighed. What had he done now?

Philomene proceeded.

'I'll jolly well tell Torquilla and — and everybody, so when that pig comes prancing out ... of all the mean, dishonest frights! Verity, indeed! Black beastly falsity, if you ask me! ... '

The Inspector sighed.

But next moment the incarnate vengeance at his side had changed again into a well-mannered little girl, who pressed him long and ardently by the hand.

'Thanks just awfully, sir. I'll never forget — and the others won't either. Now we shall be able to give that — *pig*

— what she deserves! I must go now. Good-bye.'

And Philomene was gone, running backwards across the lawn, waving her hand to the Inspector.

The Inspector sighed.

His sigh was a troubled one.

26

MORE TURTLE SOUP

Mr. Turtle was found seated in a wheelbarrow, his clay pipe in famous fume, making, so it seemed, his morning meditation.

No sooner was he aware of the Inspector's approach than he elaborately pretended not to be; he hummed a tune, puffed smoke and hitched his short legs over the side of the barrow.

'Good morning to you, Mr. Turtle . . . '

At this, with a well affected start of surprise, Mr. Turtle seemed to come back to himself.

'Mornin' to *you*, sir. Here's me believin' myself,' said Mr. Turtle, 'in maiden meditation, fancy-free!'

'A beautiful morning after the rain,' suggested the Inspector.

Mr. Turtle favoured the racy spring sunshine and pale blue sky with a tepid glance.

''Tain't too bad,' he allowed.

He crammed a finger tight into the red-hot crater of his pipe, and came to the point.

'And 'ow are you gettin' along, sir, with the 'orrible case of old Madam Sly-ema?'

'I think I am at the end of it,' the Inspector said.

Mr. Turtle slung his legs from one side of the barrow to the other before he replied.

'I 'ope it ain't Turtle as you've fixed on ultimate. Not but what if the idee an' the opportunity 'ad occurred coincidental . . . There's nobody likes better than me, sir, to see a lady come down the gardin a-sniffin' at the flowers, but when it comes to sniffin' at the gardener . . . '

He turned aside and spat.

'No, it isn't you, Mr. Turtle,' the Inspector said. 'But I'm going to ask you for your help . . . '

'Which no friend of Turtle's ever asked in vain. In what capacity can I serve you, sir? . . . '

'A familiar one, Mr. Turtle: with a spade. I propose in fact to do a little digging in the grave . . . '

Mr. Turtle showed no signs of horror or repulsion, nor did he immediately rise from the barrow.

'It's my belief, sir,' he remarked, 'as that old lady 'ad *got* to die, like . . . '

'We all have,' said the Inspector.

'That's right, sir — like the grass of the field and the sparks as flies uppards. Wot's to 'inder you and me, sir, fallin' down dead simultaneous?'

'What indeed, Mr. Turtle?'

'An' after death the judgement, sir,' said Mr. Turtle, seeming to find an uncommon relish in the prospect.

He went on:

'But which my meanin', sir, did not relate to our common mortiality, but to the partic'ler case of old Slyema. It's my belief as she come her games once too often . . . '

'Mine too, Mr. Turtle.'

'That's 'ow I reasoned it out, sir, a-settin' in this 'ere barrer, as you sees me identical. There's a sayin', sir, as even a worm will turn . . . '

'You believe,' said the Inspector, 'that

the old woman was up to some constructive devilry, and that she was murdered to stop her?'

'Gentler measures wouldn't 'ave been no use,' murmured Mr. Turtle.

He seemed to ruminate. The Inspector was just going to remind him about the spade, when he spoke again.

'Stormy weather we've been having, sir?'

'Very wet,' agreed the Inspector.

'Come down in buckets, sir!'

'Torrential indeed.'

'Not a bit o' good for dryin' clothes,' said Mr. Turtle with a shake of the head.

All this apparent irrelevance did not deceive the Inspector; he realized that in his own way Mr. Turtle was working round to a climax. It was part of the patient wisdom of the Inspector that he never tried to hurry Turtles.

With characteristic slowness Mr. Turtle began to rummage about among some vegetable oddments in his barrow.

'There's the loam on it,' he muttered, 'and the rain and pretty nigh everything but the writin'. A pretty pickle it do be in, to be sure! . . . '

'Yes?' suggested the Inspector.

For answer Mr. Turtle produced with great caution what appeared to be a sodden wad of paper and began with gingerly fingers to unfold it.

The Inspector watched him intently.

'Stuck it is,' muttered Mr. Turtle.

Finally he got the mess in some measure straightened out, and handed it to the Inspector.

'Which if it was a billy-do,' he remarked, 'it wouldn't get the courtship much forrader.'

It certainly would not!

The Inspector saw the design of the thing at once; he had no doubt that he held in his hands a duly attested and witnessed — but utterly undecipherable — Will.

'Where did you find this?' he asked.

'Which I ain't no body-snatcher, sir — Mrs. Turtle not likin' to 'ave 'em about in the 'ouse; nor yet one 'o these vampires. But find that dokyment I did, sir,' said Mr. Turtle, 'scratched deepish down in the loose earth on old Sly-ema's grave.'

'What gave you the idea of looking there?'

'I ain't a man as is badly off for idees, but this wasn't an idee. I see plain with my eyes, sir, as that grave 'ad been tampered with. I ain't a fantastical man, sir, but at first it did cross me mind as it might be old Sly-ema a'tryin' to resurrect, like, and it give me a bit of a turn. But me mind, sir, soon rejecks that superstition . . . I fetches me spade, sir, and extricates this dokyment.'

He sniffed pathetically, and wiped his nose on his shirt-sleeve.

'You're very welcome, sir, to any extra trouble it give a 'ard-workin' man.'

The Chief Inspector was by now quite sure that he held in his hand that 'evil will which was in the grave'; and he was equally sure that its malice was frustrated. It had been soaked by the rain and buried in the earth, and no expert at the Yard by any number of processes would ever be able to tell what was given and declared upon it. Why had it been buried like that? The reason for strange things is usually to be sought in the mind of strange people. Psychology notwithstanding, the mind must ever remain an unpredictable factor in human affairs.

Meanwhile here in his hand, a pulped mass, was the thing he had sought, and the whole story of the crazy but inspired crime mapped itself out under his eye.

He began to fumble in his pocket for the wherewithal to banish that pathetic look from the face of Mr. Turtle.

'Mr. Turtle, this is only a little personal tribute in acknowledgement of your — ah — admirable police work. But when the Baron Sliema comes to know, and — and ... Of course I must not take it upon myself to say, but ... '

Mr. Turtle pulled at the side-whisker which served him as a forelock.

'It is satisfaction enough, sir,' he said with simple dignity, 'to 'ave done me dooty and earned your kind thanks. Money is nothing to me, sir — '

Here he carefully stowed away the Inspector's donation in a remote pocket.

' — compared with dooty and friend-
ship. But there's no denying, sir, as times
is 'ard, and every little 'elps.'

27

THE DEAD HAND FAILS
TO STRIKE

Returning to the house with his trophy, the Inspector first again examined it himself and then dispatched it by a constable for more searching examination at the Yard.

He wondered what freak of a malign fancy that blur of obliterated ink concealed.

Probably in due time he would come to know.

Meanwhile the crime had been a complete success in so far as it was meant to thwart the dead hand. Luck had stood by the deed, and by all the clumsy and apparently gratuitous risks undertaken afterwards. The whole thing was the conception of a dim mind suddenly illuminated, and a groping purpose mysteriously sustained.

Mysteriously . . . Yes; for why had the long spell of fine, dry weather broken in storm in the very day of the funeral? But for that, the paper taken from the grave would have been a valid instrument of harm. Crauford and Venetia would be stranded; the Convent deprived of its legacy . . .

But the storm had come; the rain had descended, washing out the traces, redeeming malice from itself.

'Listen to the rain, Crauford; listen . . .'

The Inspector recalled Venetia's words with a feeling of eeriness, almost.

Truly, God was not mocked!

Crauford was lucky to be in the same boat as the Convent. It looked as if God had not meant the Convent to be deprived of those resources it would so well know how to use!

And à propos of this, the Inspector remembered a conversation he had once had with Reverend Mother.

They had been discussing the future of such a child as Inez Escapado, and he had expressed wonder as to what they could possibly hope to make of her.

Reverend Mother had replied rather sharply.

'Make of Inez? God will see to that. I should not be at all surprised if she came to us.'

'Became — a *nun!*' he had gasped.

And Reverend Mother had spoken and said:

'I see you are still wrong about nuns, Mr. Inspector. You think of them all as originally good, sweet souls, almost too feckless to do anything but warble faintly in choir. I wish I could persuade you of your mistake. Religion has always been likened to military service, and it is to strong and militant souls that its profession appeals. Do you know that nuns are among the most adventurous of mankind? They have gone all round the earth and into its worst places. They are to be found where only priests have the courage to go with them. Men do not know what the resistance of a woman is, once she believes that her service is of God . . . Can't you see Inez as a promising recruit? Can you imagine her hanging back? No, Mr. Inspector, some of the greatest saints were refractory children . . . '

She had added impressively.

'If you could see the warfare of the spirit as it really is, you would not think of Mother Trevor as a meek and gentle lady shunning all observation, but as a bright and shining figure erect in a chariot and clad in the armour of an Amazon.'

The Inspector had believed her, and he did believe her.

He brought his mind back to practical matters. How to proceed? Venetia and Crauford were out for most of the day, beginning upon the delightful task of buying the girl a trousseau. When they returned, Crauford must be told of the discovery in the grave. It would be comical to watch his reaction when he learnt how narrow had been his escape! Would he realize then who must have done the murder, and why? The Inspector did not credit him with the slightest desire to exercise his mind on any such subject. What mattered to him to the exclusion of everything else was Venetia and his forthcoming marriage.

Afterwards . . . Well, it should not be hard to get a confession when he was able to show that he knew everything already.

And afterwards again? The Inspector did not like to think of that. There would be removal from things and persons long familiar — removal to a prison infirmary . . . and, in a little while, death . . .

Not by hanging, of course . . . from already existing and incurable disease; but death in loneliness and sorrow . . .

The Inspector sighed heavily, and slumped far down in his chair.

If only death would come before! . . .

He found himself falling into that strange Convent habit of *praying* for what he wanted:

'O God, have mercy — on all us poor sinners . . . '

28

DER TOD ALS FREUND

At a certain hour every evening there falls over the entire precincts of a religious house what is called the 'Grand Silence'.

At that time all mundane tasks are put aside, all occupations prescinded; there is no speech except what must be, and that in the lowest of tones.

Lights are lowered everywhere; and those who move about do so like shadows.

The Grand Silence is not lifted until after Mass next morning.

The Inspector had found it curious to compare this custom with that prevailing in the outside world, where the solemn and beautiful withdrawal of the sun is only the beginning of a plangent artificial day. Religion can afford to stay the hand, to rest, to turn inwards, to draw about it the shadows and echoes of night; but the service of money and pleasure is insatiable and unremitting; it can never rest for fear it should think, and if it thought it would be in hell.

The Inspector was a contemplative soul by nature, and counted the day as wasted which did not include some time for silence and recollection. He had never before seen a way of life which makes a prime point of these things, but now he did see it he liked it. He had quite abandoned that delusion of the vulgar that a woman becomes a nun because she is a misfit in life or because she has been disappointed in love. It struck him now as definitely comical that people will accept the life of a stock-broker or company-promoter as natural to humanity, but not the life of a nun. It seemed to him that it is the stock-broker who is the misfit in any rational scheme of life, and surely a man must have been disappointed in every sort of love who takes to promoting companies!

These however are the mere asides of a student of life, such as every detective-officer must be.

The Grand Silence fell upon Harrington that evening, and found the Inspector in a state of having left undone the things he ought to have done. The discovery of the morning had elicited from the Yard a definite *non possumus*. The will was unreadable. The Inspector had hung about waiting for Crauford Sliema to return, and then in the end Crauford Sliema had not returned at all; he had sent Venetia home in a taxi along with so many parcels containing frivolities that Mother Peck had been disedified, and Sister Carmela had had to help upstairs with them.

In a new and fashionable hat and costume, with stockings of superlative mesh and the daintiest *chaussures*, Venetia had been obliged to make friends with the constables in the lodge as an outlet for her vivacity.

What stupid things nuns were!

The constables had been charmed, and winked broadly at one another after her departure.

Mother Peck would be glad when Venetia Gozo was out of the House. A chit, if you asked Mother Peck.

The Inspector had naturally kept out of Venetia's way!

And so the Grand Silence fell throughout the cloister, and the Inspector was left reproaching himself for shirking.

He paced up and down the floor of the Priests' Parlour, now and then taking a book from the well-filled shelves, but never holding it for long. He told himself he would do much better to go to bed . . .

But somehow he did not go to bed.

He had a queer feeling that the day's work was not over yet.

Meanwhile, the night turned chilly.

There is perhaps no chill quite so deadly as that which besets a man when he has sat up too late and thought too much. Fancies began to afflict the Inspector . . . Was there something strange abroad in the house to-night?

He went to the door, opened it, and looked out into the corridor. There was nothing to be seen or heard.

But the fancies remained.

He did not close the door after him when he went back into the room.

In the cupboard there was whisky and soda and biscuits. His nerves badly needed pulling together. He fumbled at the cupboard door, and was on the point of opening it when a sound struck his hand as with a palsy.

It came from outside the door, but to the Inspector it sounded nearer — almost at his very side . . .

It was a cry. And yet it was hardly a cry — more a whimper . . . a sound forsaken and forlorn.

If there are voices in Purgatory they would cry like that!

An infant moans like that when it has wept itself to exhaustion, and still is unheard.

In that sound, surely, was all the unconsoled misery of the world . . .

29

DER TOD ALS FREUND (Continued)

The Inspector did not hesitate; he sought no assistance. Indeed he did not know where any was to be had at that hour.

There was just one idea in his head — that cry must be traced and *staunched*.

He paused a moment out in the corridor, listening. The cry was repeated, more faintly but, if possible, even more lamentably.

It came from the Guest Rooms on the upper floor.

Once again the Inspector was mounting those stairs — once again pushing open a bedroom door . . .

The light inside was shaded with green, it was very dim, but it sufficed to show the bed and the abjectly suffering figure upon it . . .

She had raised herself and was sitting

hunched forward, the crown of her head towards the door.

It moved the Inspector to see the sparse, white hair.

At his entrance she raised herself, her face seeming to light up; even, she found strength to spread out her hands, as she cried in a voice strangely resonant and strong:

'Crauford — Crauford! I knew you would come, Crauford. Now God be praised, it is the sign of my forgiveness!'

She saw not what was but what she wished to be; she saw not the Inspector but Crauford Sliema.

The Inspector could not think how to act for the best, so he did not think; he acted upon the impulse of his heart.

He crossed the room and took the groping hands in his; he knelt beside the bed, putting his arm round her for support. He heard his own voice saying things.

'There, there, dear. That is better, isn't it? That makes you happier? . . . '

She trembled convulsively, her face shining. There was a strange strength in the grip she took of his free arm.

'The pain is — better. Your arm is so kind and strong. It is you now, Crauford, who are strong — and I so weak . . . but — but once . . . '

'Yes, dear; yes,' he murmured.

He was acting no part; he was suffering. His heart was enlarged. He felt all that Crauford Sliema might have felt had he been a different man. He looked down with unutterable compassion upon the old woman. Yes, once it had been she who was strong, and the child so weak. Her breast was shrunk and hoar now, but once it had been firm and strong, compact and beautiful, a fountain yielding the life of all mankind . . .

For a while she spoke no more — only clung to the one arm and knew the support of the other.

Then she began to speak, in that strange, strong voice which seemed to fetch its tone from nowhere.

'Crauford — my baby . . . you have not forgotten. It was to be the sign — if you came . . . All that I did I did for you . . . For her too, in a way . . . I did not hate her. I did not hate her, Crauford . . . '

'No, dear; no . . . '

'She made me promise to obey her, Crauford — her wicked will — even beyond the grave . . . And I did obey her; I did not destroy it — it is with her . . . Do not look for it. It is enough that I obeyed her — that I kept the oath she made me swear before the blessed altar of our Lord. I did not destroy the Will, Crauford; *I destroyed her!* Have they told you she is dead? . . . '

'I know it, dear; yes . . . '

'Crauford, she *had* to die. I killed her with a knife — and yet it was not I . . . Do you understand?'

The Inspector did understand.

'Promise me, Crauford — for her sake, and in the name of God, do not look for her will . . . Do not shame your mother where she is. Let what is, be.'

He heard his voice reassuring her.

She relaxed against his arm.

'Ah-h! The pain is so much better. I am dying, Crauford. Oh, my darling, do not cry. It is so much the best. It is the only thing. And yet — thank God for your sweet and gracious tears.'

The Inspector was indeed sobbing like a child.

Desultorily — speaking from time to time, clinging always to his arm — she told him more. He groped with her, half-seeing, in the dim landscape of her failing mind. He had known everything, and yet he found he had known almost nothing; so different is motive from the action into which it is liberated.

He marvelled at the strange cunning of helplessness and simplicity — at the subterfuges of a conscience most scrupulous . . .

And yet a judge would have said, and a jury found, that she acted criminally, culpably, knowing the difference between right and wrong!

Only one thing seemed really to afflict her conscience now: the entering of the sacred enclosure — the stealing of Mother Trevor's habit . . .

'*Confiteor*,' she murmured at last, '*quia peccavi nimis* . . . Crauford, they must get me a priest . . . '

But she sounded very peaceful.

She was a good Catholic, and would confess to a priest before she died; but she was a woman, and her chief longing — miraculously vouchsafed — had been to pour out her heart to — Crauford.

She murmured drowsily:

'I am not afraid. God will understand . . . '

She went off into a doze.

Allowing for the stolidity of their temperaments, the constables in the lodge were aghast at the Chief's face when he stumbled past them to use the house telephone.

It was Reverend Mother herself who heard and pieced together his incoherent message.

A minute later, she was on the spot, bringing with her Mother Infirmarian.

Mother Assistant was ringing up the Archbishop, for it was not forgotten that this was a case involving sacrilege, from which only a Bishop can absolve.

Mother Infirmarian went straight to the patient; but Reverend Mother, less stolid than the constables, lingered with the ashen-faced Inspector.

'How good God is!' she said quaintly. 'What a blessing it was you, and not the real Crauford . . . '

The hazel gleam of her eye was unmistakable as she added:

'I expect you were able to do more than just assure the old woman of the 'natural love of an infant for its nurse'?'

'I don't know what I did, Reverend Mother. I do not indeed. I don't think I did anything; I just — suffered . . . '

'Ah,' she said, 'but that is the greatest of gifts.'

He did not understand her words until a long time afterwards, but they consoled him.

He muttered abruptly:

'The case is finished. No shadow will remain. All that a policeman can ever know, I knew before she spoke. Mother Trevor's missing habit is under the mattress. Do — do you think she will want me again?'

'I do not think so. Her heart is appeased. Very soon the Viaticum of our Lord Jesus Christ will be brought her.

Your part is done — and oh how generously and well!'

She took the Inspector's hand.

'Good night, my very dear sir. Good night, and God bless you.'

30

MURDER DOES WHAT IT WILL

Old Mrs. Moss died that night, in peace of soul and rest of body, fortified with the Last Rites of the Church, and in the firm and happy belief that Crauford Sliema had grown up into the kindest and most affectionate of men.

Reverend Mother and the Archbishop were with her.

The breath had not been long gone from her body when the Archbishop said Mass for the repose of her soul; and he stayed on afterwards for breakfast, which he expressly stipulated the Inspector should take with him.

What Reverend Mother had been saying the Inspector never knew, but the Archbishop in the kindliest manner catechised him closely about his dispositions for the religious life. Catholics always find it a little difficult to believe that souls of a certain kind have never experienced a call to that life.

'Ah well,' said the Archbishop at length, 'there's all sorts of ways to heaven, Glory be to God. You will have observed, Mr. Inspector, that we aren't all saints that have been called out of the world? . . . Just ordinary people trying, and failing, and trying again. It was such folks that the Lord called in Galilee. St Peter himself was one of 'em — an obstinate, thick-headed old fisherman! Maybe some of us fall all the shorter for aiming so high, but it's a poor spirit that sees only to laugh at in that.'

He put his hand affectionately on the Inspector's shoulder.

'It's been a pleasure to meet you, sir, and to thank you. And it's my hope, as it's Reverend Mother's too, that you will become a regular 'old child' of Harrington, seeing you deserve so well of all that's in it.'

He would have shaken hands; but the Inspector, his nominal protestantism notwithstanding, was simple enough to want something more.

The Archbishop's cordial man-to-man smile instantly altered to an expression strangely different, though the smile remained. Raising his ringed hand, the great gem of which the May sunshine caught and kindled:

'*Benedico . . . in nomine Patris — et Filii — et Spiritus Sancti . . .*'

A little later Reverend Mother was in the room, seated as usual bolt upright on a hard chair. There was not about her that fugitive air, as of one briefly detained upon the wing, which there usually was; it was clear she meant to stay and hear all about everything.

And indeed she said so.

'I want to know how you worked it all out, Mr. Inspector — from the beginning, when you first came. Dear me, one talks of that as if it were a long time ago — and yet it is really only a few days!'

She composed herself to listen, which she did as one knowing *how* to listen. It is not nowadays a common accomplishment.

The Inspector could only hope his face did not give away quite all he felt.

'It will be a pleasure to tell you,' he said. And he spoke the truth.

He cleared his throat.

'Of course, when I came here — to me, too, it seems a long time ago — I had no knowledge at all of Convents or of Nuns. There was considerable prejudice against them in my mind — that kind of lazy prejudice which is so inveterate. I undertook the case with great reluctance.'

He went on, after a pause for thought:

'But we are like you in that; we have to do as we are told and — if you will pardon the expression — lump what we don't like. We also are under authority. But I will own I was nervous of being the fool who rushes in . . . '

Exactly what he meant by this he could not have said, but there was an obscure compliment lurking somewhere so he coughed and hurried on.

But for the quick intelligence of her eyes Reverend Mother might almost have been a piece of furniture, so still was she.

'I — er — well, I — expected something quite different from what I found. I found — in you all — a certain

— ah — realistic attitude. I had, I own, expected that devout ladies living aside from the world might have some difficulty in — er . . . '

'Facing facts?' Reverend Mother suggested.

'Well — that was my misgiving. It is I believe the general opinion held of nuns. It is almost an — er — dogma with many people that nuns are — introverted persons; essentially unpractical; full of a selfish desire to protect their own souls — to preserve their illusions . . . But I did try to come here with an open mind . . . I — I, so to speak . . . '

He floundered a little, but Reverend Mother restored him with a quick understanding nod; and he went on:

'Prejudice is fatal at all times. All the worst troubles of the world feed on prejudice. In a detective officer it is inexcusable; he is to judge by ascertained facts only. I had not completed my first — er — interview with yourself before I was quite sure I should find myself — not hampered but assisted . . . '

Reverend Mother allowed a little of the

gratification she felt to shine in her deeply attentive eyes.

The Inspector felt rather than saw the light.

'I saw I need not fear lack of — really helpful — co-operation. I saw that you also put facts in the first place.' He smiled slightly, and went on:

'You warned me that nuns are not saints, and that I must expect to find in the cloister much that I am familiar with in the world. Quite so; yet it was not very long before I had completely excluded the Community from my list of possibles.'

He looked at Reverend Mother rather triumphantly. She returned his look with steady gravity. All she said was, 'Yes? . . . '

'Murder,' the Inspector proceeded, 'is a liberation of the ego. Anybody might commit a murder in certain circumstances. But this murder was committed in the chapel — in the presence of the — ah — Sacrament of the altar. I did not think, upon reflection, that any *nun* would commit *sacrilege*. The *locus* of the crime excluded the Community.'

It was impossible to tell anything from

Reverend Mother's face except that she was listening with deep interest.

The Inspector resumed, with another smile:

'In spite of little Inez and the truly frightful story you arranged for me to hear — '

At this Reverend Mother did definitely glitter.

' — I did not think it was one of the children. Murder in a child would almost certainly not be without antecedent symptoms, and none was recorded. I asked many questions but heard nothing at all suggestive.'

He added quickly:

'In fact, from the very first I was sure that either Mrs. Moss must be guilty, or Venetia Gozo must.'

Inspector as he was, and noted for his powers of observation, he could make nothing of Reverend Mother's face — at which he ventured to glance. Was she merely hearing from him what she had long known for herself? It was impossible to say. Her clear, alert eyes, with their occasional glitter of mirth, were also profoundly cryptic. If ever the Inspector saw a woman consummately able to keep a secret, he saw one in Reverend Mother.

He went on:

'Of these two I naturally inclined towards Miss Gozo. She was young and strong, and she seemed to be of a peculiar, repressed temperament. I knew at that time of no motive she could have — but there is such a thing as sheer hatred; and I strongly suspected that Madame Sliema had been trying the patience of her dependents beyond the line of safety. It was a significant trait in the old woman that she was in the habit of composing ribald wills. I formed the hypothesis that it had been in her mind to disinherit her son altogether and the Convent as well, and in such a way as to inflict a maximum of disappointment and mortification upon both.'

Verity would have been glad to hear what followed next.

'I was greatly helped in narrowing the field,' pursued the Inspector, 'by the clue of the torn veil. In itself it was not much, but it led to my seeing and handling the whole garment; and as soon as I had done that I was able to connect it at once with the — ah — Guest House.'

Reverend Mother's sensitive eyebrows momentarily escaped her control. 'That was surely remarkable,' she said.

'Not so much as might appear. I am naturally gifted' — here the Inspector hesitated — 'with a delicate sense of — ah — smell. I have cultivated this gift, and it has proved useful to me in establishing many associations. The veil was definitely — er — impregnated with an *odour* (entirely inoffensive) which I had noted in the Guest House. Surely,' he broke off, 'you must have detected this ah — aroma — yourself?'

Reverend Mother shook her head with a certain sadness.

'I am afraid,' she said, 'I am definitely one of the 'fallen sons of Eve' . . . You remember Chesterton's poem about the dog? I never noticed anything except that the place was abominably fusty . . . Old Madame would never have a window opened on any account.'

'It is just a natural gift,' said the

Inspector apologetically and yet with some mild pride. 'It is often a great puzzle, for nothing is so difficult to identify as a smell. This one was quite accidentally revealed to me by Sister Carmela . . . It was Maltese Orange Flower Water. Apparently the old lady imported the ingredients from Malta and made them up for herself.'

Reverend Mother nodded. 'Yes, Sister Cook has often complained, poor dear soul! But while I deeply sympathised, I am afraid I never inquired.'

'That clue practically proved to me,' went on the Inspector, 'that whoever did this mysterious creeping about at night — in disguise — came from the Guest House. Of course I had no notion as yet why, but that only showed that the underlying psychology of the crime was still unknown to me.'

'How reasonable!' Reverend Mother sighed. It was a wistful, even self-reproachful sigh, as of one greatly admiring and wanting to imitate the spirit which the words denoted. It was charac-teristic of Reverend Mother that she sought examples everywhere and laid them intimately to heart.

The Inspector had resumed:

'The next event of importance was of course the arrival on the scene of Crauford Sliema. As soon as it became known that he and Miss Gozo were engaged, my suspicions of Miss Gozo were naturally strengthened. Her motive was now plain, if it could be shown that she was aware of the altered will. I set to work to make a case against Miss Gozo.'

It was now the Inspector's turn to sigh, which he did heavily. The thought of Venetia was still a deep reproach to him, and he would have to tell Reverend Mother of the fiasco which had resulted from his mistaken deductions.

'I blame myself,' he said, 'for not realizing that being in love accounts for many of the — er — characteristics I had noted in Miss Gozo. I have found in my experience that one so often overlooks the *ordinary* things. The case against Mrs. Moss was quite clear — allowing for its inherent improbabilities. I forgot to be on my guard against confusing the improbable and the impossible. I allowed myself to be prejudiced against Miss Gozo. I repeat,' said the Inspector, with another sigh, 'I had no right to be deflected from the evidence against Mrs. Moss. Mr. Turtle had practically clinched that.'

'Turtle!' The exclamation was wrung from Reverend Mother.

'He had fixed beyond doubt,' said the Inspector, 'that someone entered St. Joseph's chapel at 5.22. His watch — an heirloom, he tells me — is a very accurate time-keeper.'

'Yes, I know that watch,' said Reverend Mother.

'This exact fixing of the time,' went on the Inspector, 'made a hole in Mrs. Moss's alibi. The thought crossed my mind that Mrs. Moss could, on occasion, get about very much more quickly than anybody supposed. On the negative side, too, Mr. Turtle's evidence was conclusive against Mrs. Moss'.

'On the negative side?' Reverend Mother queried.

'The figure he observed in the cloister,'

the Inspector said, '*could be nobody else but Mrs. Moss*'.

But Reverend Mother was not easily to be convinced by evidence, negative or positive, which rested on the testimony of Mr. Turtle, and the Inspector had to spend some time in explaining to her. Even when he had finished, Reverend Mother would only say, 'H'm!' in a distinctly snubbing manner.

'I suppose,' she remarked, 'it never crossed your mind that Turtle himself might have done it?'

'I naturally considered the point — as he was the last person known to have been in the chapel; but, upon consideration, I dismissed Mr. Turtle.'

Reverend Mother looked as if she wished she could do the same thing.

The Inspector proceeded, with another sigh and general relapse into melancholy.

'But my prejudice against Miss Gozo was too strong. I allowed myself to be deflected from the only established facts. In a very interesting conversation which I managed to have with Mrs. Moss on the day of the funeral I formed the conclusion that to her the crime seemed like an act of God. This I thought pointed not to guilt but to mental confusion. I was a fool not to see that guilt is quite compatible with mental confusion about being guilty. 'God struck her down' — those were the very words — 'and her evil Will is in the grave with her'. Now, in fact, at that time the Will was not in the grave. I remember she hesitated. I did not grasp the point; I took her to mean that Madame Sliema was dead and her evil intentions were dead with her. She practically told me the whole story then, but I had no ears to hear with. I was so full of prejudice against Miss Gozo.'

He looked at Reverend Mother in a manner she was familiar with — that of a culprit making unwilling admission. She encouraged him with a smile. In spite of the smile he swallowed hard before proceeding.

'That same night the ah — ghost — walked again. With a promptitude beyond all praise you and your admirable Community turned out in pursuit. I proceeded to ah — rush — upon my doom. I ah — entered — Miss Gozo's bedroom, in the full belief that she was absent . . . '

He dropped his voice to a hoarse whisper, adding:

'She was *not* absent.'

He dared not glance at Reverend Mother, and went on miserably:

'My presence in her bedroom naturally much upset the young lady. I was ah — myself — considerably upset. It was a situation of the utmost delicacy. I have ah — found it — extremely difficult even to mention such a thing to a lady of your profession . . . '

He broke off; he all but broke down. Until Reverend Mother spoke he could say nothing more.

And for a minute Reverend Mother did not speak — could not perhaps have spoken without her voice betraying her. Now she understood why the Inspector had refused to eat his sausages the following morning! It moved her heart to think how almost piteously virtuous some men are, in spite of the reputation of the sex as a whole. When she spoke at last, it was in a most matter-of-fact voice.

'My dear Mr. Inspector, don't you greatly exaggerate a very trifling mistake arising out of your duty?'

The Inspector at this point ventured to raise his eyes, and was almost shocked to find that Reverend Mother was not looking shocked in the very least.

'Nobody,' pursued Reverend Mother with emphasis, 'could ever suspect you of anything but a single-minded purpose to do your duty.'

The Inspector was rallying like a refreshed geranium, but he still accused himself.

'A man is never so wrong,' he mumbled, 'as when he acts upon prejudice . . . '

'And a man is never so much a man,' countered Reverend Mother, 'as when he admits it.' She added quickly, but not so quickly as to sound abrupt:

'Go on telling me about poor old Mrs. Moss. It is quite marvellous how you entered into the riddle of her mind.'

'I took her at her literal word after that,' the Inspector said. 'There had been such a Will as the one I had always supposed, and it was *in the grave* with its maker. I had only to dig, and I should find the evidence. I had only to search, and I should find the incriminating habit.'

Reverend Mother nodded. 'It was under the mattress, poor old soul,' she said.

The Inspector sighed. 'Yes, her strength failed her, and she had no time to get rid of it again.'

He went on:

'I had now, in our police sense, a case. I could apply for a warrant. But the thought of removing that poor old woman to a prison infirmary — '

Reverend Mother nodded.

'I *prayed*,' the Inspector said, 'here in this parlour I *prayed* to be spared so unkind a duty . . . '

Again Reverend Mother nodded.

'Of course,' said the Inspector, 'I still could not *account for* the crime. Why had Mrs. Moss been at such pains to preserve the Will which it was her interest to destroy? But for the rain, that Will might have been — would have been — unearthed and proved, and the murder done in vain. Why had the worm turned, only to turn tail again? Some complex of a bewildered mind? — yes, but therefore all the more difficult to understand and bring to light. You know Daudet's story of the Pope's mule, which kept its kick for ten years? Mrs. Moss had kept hers for nearer thirty, and would most likely have kept it for ever if Madame Sliema had not, so to speak, *asked for it*. All Mrs. Moss's humiliated maternal feelings, all her loyalty to you here at Harrington, were stirred at last, and the feeble old minion definitely sentenced her tyrant to die. She must die — and soon — at once — while Mrs. Moss was still alive to avert the consequences of her malignity.'

Reverend Mother pondered. 'To think,' she said, 'that the old woman had it in her!'

'Old women have a great deal in them,' the Inspector said, 'and are less afraid of consequences than young ones. What was all the witch business but fear of what old women have in them? A purpose once formed in a mind like that, and it becomes the pearl of great price. Madame Sliema revived self-respect in her old retainer — to her own undoing. Murder may be made to seem beautiful — heroic — tender . . . '

Reverend Mother's way of listening was more heartening than applause, and the Inspector began to find himself at his best.

'It sounds a dreadful thing — the idea is strange and dreadful — but the fixed purpose of killing Madame Sliema and so at long last of asserting herself became a new principle of life to Mrs. Moss. She desired to take life in the same degree as a woman might desire to give it. Madame Sliema, suspecting nothing, was not discreet no doubt; she rubbed her intentions well in on Mrs. Moss. It is rather horrible to think of those two old women sitting together, the one trumpeting her spite, the other nursing her darling purpose. But spite is never discreet, or we should have fewer lawsuits; spite is always in a mood of triumph, and feels the need of boasting itself. Day after day Madame Sliema insulted Mrs. Moss by insulting Crauford and laughed coarsely at her affection for him.

'What I am going to suggest now,' he went on, 'is mainly conjecture. We are groping about in very foggy places. The thought of killing Madame Sliema revived self-respect in Mrs. Moss, and the thought of having the Will in her possession gave her — what she had never had before — a sense of power. Not power in the vulgar sense of blackmail, but in the far more subtle, exquisite — one might even use the word *voluptuous* — in the voluptuous sense of being a benevolent providence to those she loved. Power, when you have never had any and never expected to have any, is like an intoxication; it acts on the higher brain centres and liberates repression. I may be mistaken, but I can only account for Mrs. Moss's risky escapades of dressing up the way she did, on the theory that doing so renewed the ecstasy of the blow dealt in the chapel . . . '

'And ministered,' Reverend Mother

suggested, 'to this new sense of power?'

'Exactly,' replied the Inspector. 'We shall never understand this crime unless we realize that the whole thing had for Mrs. Moss a definitely delightful character. She could easily have destroyed that Will at once, but she did not want to; she wanted to possess it — to feast her eyes on it — to exult over the impotence of its maker. That I am sure is why she acted in the strange way she did. One has to think of her in her new and exultant mood of power: her almost lifelong tyrant is dead; everybody is aghast; the police are coming . . . and, in the centre of it all, solely responsible, alone in the secret, is she. She is conscious as yet of no fear either of God or man; she only knows that at last she has struck back and achieved power. It amuses her now to keep up her old character before you all, to seem weak and feeble-minded; it is all part of a grim and delicious joke. She soon develops that invariable illusion of the power-urge that God is on her side. Her behaviour with the Will is like a kitten playing with its first mouse; almost she will let it escape for the rapture of clawing it again. The poetic justice of her final disposal of it has for her the beatitude of artistic creation. She is old, remember; she has not to face a lifetime of remorse.'

He added, almost dreamily:

'I am an abstemious man by nature, but I have been — ah — drunk. I know the sense of liberation . . . while it lasts, nothing matters — nothing . . . '

'Me too,' Reverend Mother said with the greatest simplicity. 'In my youth, before I entered . . . '

'You did not enter,' the Inspector ventured to ask, 'straight from school?'

'Oh dear me, no. As I sometimes tell the children, I was not *born* in a habit. Some people tend to think one was, you know.'

The Inspector nodded his approval. 'I should think it is better to er — enter — later . . . after some little experience . . . '

But Reverend Mother would not allow that. 'These things differ with different souls. We believe it is God who acts. The time to enter is when that action no longer admits of doubt.'

'But,' hesitated the Inspector, 'how to be sure? . . . when one is so very young and inexperienced? . . .'

'There is advice to be had,' Reverend Mother said. 'A true vocation declares itself in many ways. Besides, there is a long probation. People seem to think we welcome everybody with open arms; but of course we do nothing of the kind. Why should we? What community ever wanted to be hampered with unsuitable people? If the world would only credit religion with just a little ordinary commonsense!'

She broke off in that quick but not abrupt way of hers, to say:

'And when do you think a sense of what she had done came back to Mrs. Moss?'

The Inspector answered grimly.

'When the pain came back. When that came back, she wanted no longer vengeance, no longer power — she wanted . . . love . . .'

He went on very slowly:

'I have only an inkling of her love-story. She told me it herself when she thought I was Crauford. She was ah — cynically — betrayed in early life, and she had that child whose death made her eligible for the post with Madame Sliema. The only love she had ever known in her life was first that selfish lie, and then — the fractious dependence of an ailing infant not her own. I fear Crauford was not affectionate, yet in her extremity of need she turned to him. She told me that his appearance was — the sign — of God's forgiveness . . . It was not Crauford, but — but to her it — seemed a miracle of grace . . . '

'And of course it was,' Reverend Mother said. She had produced a handkerchief — a real Convent handkerchief, several times larger than the largest man's. She added as she did so:

'I find this weather catarrhal. What a scourge this catarrh is! I hope you are immune, Mr. Inspector?'

'By no means,' answered the Inspector gravely. 'I am much subject to violent fits of sneezing.'

He also produced his handkerchief, and with it his notebook, full of the tracks of waltzing fleas, some passages of which he seemed to review with a certain wistfulness of expression. He spoke heavily.

'That is my case, Reverend Mother. I must, of course, report fully at the Yard, but there will be no sensation — no publicity . . . I can promise that . . .'

He closed his notebook and put it back in his pocket. He got up from his chair.

Reverend Mother had also risen. As the Inspector sadly perceived, she was once more on the wing. It is so in Convents; there is no lingering once necessary business is done.

She was speaking:

'I cannot easily say what I feel. It is not only your clearing up of this case . . . it is the sympathy, the understanding, you have shown of our circumstances, our way of life. You have been a true friend' — she offered her hand — 'and I thank you from my heart on behalf of us all . . .'

It was all over, the Inspector thought inwardly; there was nothing left for him to do but take himself off back to the unflowering Yard. His position here, which he had so much enjoyed — his intercourse with all these pleasant, intelligent, friendly people — it was all at an end. It never could come again. It is a terrible drawback in life, and will no doubt remit some purgatory, to be like the Inspector and get really fond of people in a short time . . . people upon whom one has no least claim. The Inspector was not a young man, and this was not by any means the first time he had experienced desolation at parting. But this he did feel was the worst time. And how like the infinite caprice of life! — of all things and of all places, to find oneself walled up in a Convent! *Le coeur est bien là . . .*

But except for an even greater measure of his old-fashioned and not a little quaint bow over the hand which Reverend Mother offered him, he said nothing until she was at the door. Then he stayed her flight.

'If,' he murmured, 'I might ask a favour . . . ?'

Swift in flight as she had been, at this

her wings seemed to furl, and she was all attention.

'It is only — ' he began; then broke off, and began again.

'It is a matter of very slight importance. I have long cherished ah — literary — ambitions, in my spare time. I have not much of that. But recently I have been successful in completing a short work — a mere monograph — dealing with some observed and *felt* aspects of life in the ah — country. I have a cottage in the Cotswolds. The ah — work — is a trifle, and owes its publication entirely to my name as a policeman.' He smiled a little forlornly. 'But I think,' he went on, 'that you ladies might ah — recognize — some of the thoughts, and I am wondering if you would ah — permit — the dedication to — er — yourself and the Community at Harrington?'

He seemed unaffectedly doubtful.

Reverend Mother was deeply touched; the something lonely, pathetic and lovable in the speaker struck her, not for the first time. So he had a cottage in the Cotswolds! She was glad, and had no difficulty in picturing his grave and meditative potterings about the garden. And then his book of most unpoliceman-like thoughts worked out laboriously but with how much pleasure in that spare time of which he had so little! And now his wanting to dedicate this treasure of his heart to Harrington because he believed the thoughts would be 'recognized' there!

Her voice in answering the Inspector was very gracious and cordial indeed, and her clear smile was very bright.

'You call that a favour. We shall look upon it very differently. If you would like to dedicate your book to us here at Harrington, we shall be honoured. We shall read it, and I am sure we shall — recognize — many of the thoughts. May I, on our side, ask a favour?'

The Inspector mumbled something which might have meant anything.

'If you can spare time to ring up,' Reverend Mother said, 'may we hope that you will bring us the book in person? Remember what the Archbishop said. We should all like to be able to look forward to seeing you again.'

'You are too kind,' muttered the Inspector.

But Reverend Mother definitely did not think so.

Epilogue:

FINIS CORONAT OPUS

Later that same day Reverend Mother said to Mother Peagle:

'Do you know, Mother, I have a feeling I've forgotten something . . . '

'No wonder, Reverend Mother; with all this anxiety and extra work . . . '

'Something,' said Reverend Mother; 'which I was just on the point of doing when all this rumpus began.'

'So long ago . . . ' said Mother Peagle.

'Not really, you know, Mother; it is only a few days really. Now what can it have been that I was going to do? I know it was something important . . . '

Mother Peagle looked sympathetic.

'Try not thinking about it, dear Reverend Mother, and then it will suddenly pop into your mind.'

'But I want it to pop now. Ah!' cried Reverend Mother. 'I've got it! Of course,

Mother: it was just after Benediction, don't you remember? and that incorrigible Verity Goodchild had come in late and caused a disturbance. I was just going to give her a good scolding. Of course, of course. Please tell her to come to me at once.'

'Oh but, Reverend Mother,' pleaded Mother Peagle, 'if you will permit me . . . It is all some time ago now, and Verity has been such a good girl. And you remember how plucky she was that night when — '

'Please, Mother, tell her to come to me.'

Verity, long discharged from the infirmary and in perfect union again with Philomene and her other friends with and without Ribbons, heard the summons and the reason for it with amazed disgust.

'Well, of all the pigs!' she exclaimed, when Mother Peagle had gone. 'Fancy letting the sun go up and down on your wrath like that! It's practically a mortal sin, and I wouldn't have believed it even of Reverend Mother.'

The others all agreed that for sheer

cold-blooded, relentless malice Reverend Mother was the bee's whiskers and the cat's very own pyjamas.

'All this time after,' Verity said, as she quickly tidied her hair, 'and after all I've done for the Convent! Catch me doing it again! I wouldn't stir hand or foot if I knew for a fact there was a bomb under Reverend Mother's stall in chapel!'

The others agreed and condoled.

'Quite right! I'm sure I don't blame you! Talk about Christian charity! . . . Why, a heathen is a saint compared with Reverend Mother . . . '

Philomene wept with rage.

It was still the Lady month of May, with its daily Benediction, and the bell announcing this ceremony was just beginning to sound over far and near when Verity went in to Reverend Mother. But Reverend Mother could do wonders with minutes; and Verity was out again, and veiled, and in her place in chapel, and praying really quite hard, and in that sensitive frame of mind when one's faults do really strike one as a 'bit thick' — long before the white-brocaded priest approached the altar, with his acolyte seraph tossing a smoking bowl.

We do hope that you have enjoyed reading this large print book.

Did you know that all of our titles are available for purchase?

We publish a wide range of high quality large print books including:

Romances, Mysteries, Classics
General Fiction
Non Fiction and Westerns

Special interest titles available in large print are:

The Little Oxford Dictionary
Music Book, Song Book
Hymn Book, Service Book

Also available from us courtesy of Oxford University Press:

Young Readers' Dictionary
(large print edition)
Young Readers' Thesaurus
(large print edition)

For further information or a free brochure, please contact us at:

Ulverscroft Large Print Books Ltd.,
The Green, Bradgate Road, Anstey,
Leicester, LE7 7FU, England.
Tel: (00 44) **0116 236 4325**
Fax: (00 44) **0116 234 0205**

Other titles in the
Linford Mystery Library:

THE RED TAPE MURDERS

Gerald Verner

Superintendent Budd's latest murder investigation begins with the murder of a solicitor, found strangled with red tape. Soon, two more local solicitors are murdered in similar fashion. Eventually Budd learns that two years earlier, a man shot himself when about to lose the bungalow he built, under a compulsory purchase order of the council. Two of the solicitors had acted in the sale of the land, and the third had acted for the council. Is someone seeking vengeance for the man who committed suicide — himself a victim of red tape?